Mer~ ~ne.

Meredetn sat straight up in bed. Will was gone. Why hadn't he told her he was leaving so soon? Was it such a big secret? Don't write notes, he had said. Destroy this letter. Trust him. *Oh, Will, what are you involved in that must be hidden?*

"William Castleton, don't you dare be a British spy or I. . .I'm afraid I will be left with a totally broken heart. First Matt and now this!"

She threw the letter from her as hard as she could, but a brisk morning breeze wafted it back to the coverlet. After stretching to reclaim the bit of parchment, she jerked the Starfire quilt up over her head. Muted sobs shook the bedclothes until all her despair and frustration drained away. Only the loneliness was left.

ALICE ALLEN's home is in Kansas with her husband Bill. They have a close-knit family of three grown children and four grandchildren. Alice hopes to reach both children and adults with God's truth through her writings, which include curriculum, plays, poems, and more.

The Starfire Quilt

Alice Allen

Heartsong Presents

I would like to dedicate this book to my family, who encouraged and never doubted; to Rebecca Germany and Tracie Peterson, for all their patient help; and to all Christians who walk through both the happy and the worrisome paths of this world, trusting in the Lord God to provide a way and to walk through it with them.
God bless you all.

A note from the author:
I love to hear from my readers! You may write to me at the following address: **Alice Allen**
       Author Relations
       P.O. Box 719
       Uhrichsville, OH 44683

ISBN 1-57748-275-1

THE STARFIRE QUILT

Cover illustration by Kay Salem.

PRINTED IN THE U.S.A.

one

September 12, 1777

Fair Lady sailed effortlessly over the stone fence and thundered into the meadow. The surrounding woods were just beginning to show glorious fall colors. Pulling up on the reins, Meredeth Elliott headed for the shade of the trees. Heat had already dampened her linen shirt and flecked her horse's neck with perspiration.

"Oh, Matt, why haven't we heard from you? I miss you so much," she said as she gazed ahead.

A snort from Fair Lady was the only warning when, from the cover of the trees, a blaze-faced sorrel came pounding straight for them, its rider hunched low over the horse's head.

"Why, he's trying to run us down!" Meredeth screamed.

As survival reaction overcame shock, Meredeth turned her mount's lead and dug her heels into the horse's sides. Fair Lady responded promptly, but there was so little time as the big sorrel brushed past and then sped off across the field. By the time Meredeth had eased Fair Lady to a stop, the intruder had disappeared from view.

Swiftly dismounting, the petite rider checked her mare for injuries. Fair Lady limped a few steps, then halted and nuzzled Merry's shoulder.

"The brute! Whatever was he thinking of to careen into us like that?"

Gently she touched the mare's flank and leg. "I think it's only a strain, but we'd better walk you back to the stables. Jeremiah will know if there is any serious harm done."

With an angry glance in the direction that the retreating horse had taken, Merry reached for her bonnet. There, on the ground,

5

she noticed a package wrapped in brown paper. Frowning, she slowly picked it up and turned it around in her hands.

"Could that rider have dropped this? But why?" Dejected, Merry started for home.

Jeremiah Grundy saw her coming and loped toward her. "Did she ketch a hoof in a hole, Miss Meredeth?"

"No, she didn't. Jeremiah, have you seen strangers about lately?"

"No'm. Cain't say I have," he responded solemnly as he leaned to inspect the damage.

"A rider on a big sorrel came racing out of the woods near the meadow. He'd have knocked us flat if I hadn't turned Fair Lady. I think he did graze her, but you'd better check her carefully."

"I surely will, Miss Meredeth."

Merry gave her horse a pat of reassurance, then ran for the house and hurried up the back stairs to her room. Instead of changing her clothes, she sat for several minutes and examined the packet. With thin-lipped decisiveness, she tore the paper off and out fell a minuscule parcel of linen squares, each with a set of numbers inked onto it. Beneath was a folded parchment. In spite of shaking hands, she opened and read the letter.

> *Dear Merry,*
>
> *I hope you receive this as it will be my last letter to you. Someone's been following me. I have only one sheet of parchment. The squares cut from my shirt are for General Washington, who is in the Philadelphia area. Please get them to him as soon as you can. Find John Clark or Charles Craig. They will know what to do. Don't talk about this to anyone else.*
>
> *I love you and Papa.*
>
> *For freedom!*
> *Matt*

Meredeth sat stunned, the linen squares clutched in her hands. Tears fell, but they could not wash away the possible meaning of his message.

"Oh, Matt, I can't believe you might be dead. With Papa in Philadelphia that would leave me alone, except for Aunt Mina. She's a dear, but her mind functions on only two subjects: food and the latest fashions. I need your encouragement and steady strength."

Such small snippets of cloth to be so important! That thought slammed Meredeth right back to the monstrous problem at hand. *Now I must get them to the Patriots. How am I going to do that?*

"Oh, dear Lord, guide me," she whispered. "I want to help, yet I have no idea how to do this."

"Merry love, luncheon is all set out for us," Aunt Mina called up the stairs.

"I'll be right there, Aunt Mina, as soon as I put things in order."

Hastily she racked her brain for a secure hidey-hole. The sewing basket on the work table! What better place to conceal small bits of linen? She snipped threads holding the lining in place along one side of the basket to make an opening long enough to insert the cloth pieces.

A quick glance in the mirror confirmed that, as usual, tendrils of her red-gold hair had loosened from their pins. She took time to smooth her hair and add a few pins. Then, tugging her skirts into place, she hurried down the stairs.

"Did you enjoy your ride, my dear?" Aunt Mina glanced briefly at her niece.

Meredeth caught the soft "tsk" of reproach, but after grace was said, the food claimed all of her aunt's attention, and Meredeth hoped she might forget to chide her for coming to the table in riding clothes.

Indeed, Aunt Mina was full of gossip, with which she eagerly enlightened Meredeth throughout the meal. Somehow Merry responded in the right places, though her mind raced ahead, planning. When her aunt's chatter subsided for a moment, Merry plunged in.

"Tomorrow we should make a trip to Philadelphia. I hear there is a new shipment of fabric available at the linen drapers'. We need long cloth for bed gowns, some silk for ribands, and perhaps a bit of lace."

"That sounds delightful, Merry. What time do you want to leave?" Aunt Mina asked.

"I'll order the coach for seven tomorrow morning. That will get us to town before ten. While I'm down at the stables, you can take your nap and I can exercise Papa's stallion."

As soon as Meredeth could excuse herself, she hurried to the stables and, once in the meadow, she let Othello, her father's horse, have his head. Taking the bit eagerly, Othello pranced a few paces, then settled into a steady canter.

"I feel better doing something, even if it doesn't ease the ache in my heart. Should I tell Papa about Matt? But no, Matt said not to mention it to anyone else, except John Clark or Charles Craig."

The sound of hoofbeats close behind pierced her mental detachment and, with every nerve on edge, she slowed Othello to a trot and swung him slightly to the left. She realized that the approaching horse was not the same one that had almost run them down, and she relaxed a bit. This beautiful horse was all of sixteen hands at least, and the man atop the horse was also large, had wide shoulders, and was sitting on his mount as if he had been carved there.

When they were within easy speaking distance, the rider lifted his hat in greeting, revealing dark hair worn a bit long but well groomed. The sun added gold flecks as his head bent in a slight bow.

"My lady, I am ashamed to admit I have been led astray by the beauty of this area. Can you tell me, please, whose land this is?"

"You are in Cresswick Manor Acres, owned by my father, Dr. Lawrence Elliott. What manor are you seeking, sir?"

"Oliver Moreland invited several of his friends to a house party, but as it is difficult for me to remain indoors on such a lovely day, I decided to go for a ride. My horse, Ahmed, was as anxious as I for a run."

"He shows his heritage. He carries that proud head like a prince."

"He is a prince, a foal of Queen Serenay."

Merry's gaze shifted from the horse to the stranger and his fathomless pair of dark blue eyes. *This man is a charmer and he knows it.* That thought brought a warmth to her cheeks.

Chagrined at her obvious response, she turned her face away as she said, "There's a path through this end of the trees that will take you back to Moreland's. I'm sure you will have no trouble finding it."

"I thank you, my lady. William Castleton, at your service. If you are ever lost on my land, or anywhere else for that matter, my specialty is helping damsels in distress." With that, the great horse swiveled at his master's touch and loped away.

"His specialty! Well of all the conceited, arrogant dunderheads!"

At this emotional outburst, Othello sidestepped and it took all of Merry's strength to calm the animal. By the time she raised her eyes to the woods, the stranger was gone.

"And good riddance," she mumbled. "We are in the midst of a war and he attends house parties."

Suddenly she realized how strange it was to have encountered two strangers within hours of each other, and that made her lose all desire to ride any farther that day. Turning, she headed back to the stables.

At table that evening Meredeth did not mention either encounter. There were other decisions to be made, and if any more of that house party lost themselves, they could just talk to the stable lads. She certainly needed no strangers in her life at present. It was complicated enough already. The idea of getting away for a few days pleased her.

❧

When Merry, Aunt Mina, and their maids, Anna and Dela, climbed into the traveling chaise the next morning, wispy ghosts of fog haunted the countryside. Merry stared out, unseeing, as they rumbled along the veiled landscape. Aunt Mina and the maids settled in for a few hours' relaxation. Fortunately they did not require Meredeth's attention.

Should she tell her papa about Matt? Her last memory picture of her parent was that of a weary man, surrounded by pallets of injured; months of serving at the hospital had taken their toll. No. She would stop by the hospital, perhaps bringing him a big meat pie filled with ham and sauerkraut. She still could not believe that Matt might be dead, and it would be cruel to burden her father with that possibility when he was already inundated with wounded soldiers.

"In case the British come as far as Philadelphia," Aunt Mina said with loud determination, "I think we should move to Cousin Ferdy's. His manor is rather hidden away in the hills. Don't you think we'd be safe there, Meredeth?"

"If Washington holds Philadelphia, we won't have that problem," Merry said, sagging back into her corner.

It had been only a year since independence was declared, and already the British had taken Boston and New York. Most folks expected Philadelphia to be the next target. Could that be the information Matt was sending with those bits of linen? Nervously she clutched her reticule tighter; the small mound that those linen pieces made was not enough to be obvious.

"Halt!" someone shouted.

"May the Lord preserve us. Is it a road bandit?" Aunt Mina gasped, clutching the opal pin fastened to her woolen cloak.

"There's two men. Why one of them is Jemy Prentis," Dela, Aunt Mina's maid, said.

Meredeth and her maid, Anna, turned in their seats to see what caused the delay.

With an angry scowl, Jeremiah Grundy, their coach driver,

swung down. Chin to chin with the lanky young man on the road, Grundy spoke in unconcealed contempt. "Just what'r you up to, Jemy? There's no need for you to stop honest folk on this road."

"Gotta do it, Jeremiah. It's orders. Honest. The Brits have taken Chadd's Ford and word is they're headin' east."

"East?"

"Yessir, Mr. Grundy, toward Philadelphia."

"How soon do they 'spect they'll git there, Jemy?"

"Don't know. Washington's trying to hold them at the ford. That young Frenchie, Layfay. . .somethin', is helpin' him. No tellin' how long they can hold out."

"We're headin' for Philadelphia," Grundy advised. "Think we can make it?"

"It'd be better than goin' back to Cresswick," Jemy said.

"I'll see what Miz Elliott wants to do. Don't rightly like havin' a coachload of women on the road if the Brits are near." With that, Jeremiah walked back to the carriage, doffed his cap, and informed his passengers of the problem.

Meredeth did not hesitate to respond. "Step up the pace and make a run for it," she ordered. "We'll be safer there than at the manor. Surely General Washington won't let them take Philadelphia."

"You want I should send word back home?" Jeremiah asked.

"Yes, if it's possible. Mrs. Tulley and Barnabas could hide the silver and send the stock back to Cousin Ferdy's. I don't want to lose Fair Lady or Othello."

"Yes'm. I'll tell Jemy. He'll see to it."

After a quick word with the young man, the coachman leaped to his perch and clucked the team into action. In less than an hour, the exhausted horses swirled into the courtyard of Conners Inn, causing a tempest of dust.

"Mistress, do ya mind if'n I go see what the news is here?" Jeremiah asked as he helped the women down.

Smiling, Meredeth sent him on his way then herded her aunt and the maids into the common room, where Elijah

Conners was leaning over his counter to greet them warmly.

"Just sign right there, Miz Elliott. I'll send Poll up to fix rooms for ya. Yer pa is in the second room, left. Don't see 'im much, but that's where he keeps his clothes."

"I'll stop by to see him after I find a friend of Matt's," Meredeth said. "Have you seen John Clark or Charles Craig in town this morn?"

Conners thoughtfully tapped a long pipe stem against his chin. "Wal now, lessee. Reckon the major will be up at the Thompson-Neely place and I heard Craig was riding south a ways. If ya want to reach him, ya oughta catch Jim Hanks when he comes for his lunch at City Tavern. In fact, he might be there now. Tell ya what. I'll call back to Zeke an' find out where he's headed. He might take ya there."

Zeke, the inn's ostler, offered them a ride as far as Walnut and Second, where he had a delivery. "Be ready ta leave in 'bout ten to fifteen minutes, Miz Elliott. You and Anna kin wait on the dock."

Clutching cloaks tightly against a gusty north gale, Merry and Anna watched loaders place the last few rows of boxes on Zeke's wagon. Next to them, a brewer's dray was already loaded with kegs and two men were attempting to tie a piece of oiled cloth over the lot. The sound of an angry voice turned Merry's head toward them.

"Thet keg done slipped, it has!" one of the men yelled as he danced about, holding up his wounded foot, while his companion leaned over to examine the injury. Meanwhile, the runaway keg tumbled across the wooden planks of the dock.

"Miss Merry, look out!" Anna screamed, pushing her mistress forward and getting herself out of the way of the rolling keg. But Anna's foot slipped and, with a sharp crack, her head hit a post and then she collapsed in a silent heap.

Merry was struggling to pick herself up when she heard a voice ask, "May I be of assistance? You look very much like a damsel in distress."

That lazy drawl was simply too much. Hands on hips, a

blistering setdown on her lips, Merry turned around and found herself looking at the gentleman who was too busy attending parties to fight a war.

"Is he botherin' you, Miz Merry?" Zeke inquired. Pushing Merry back, Zeke stuck his pointed beard right into Castleton's chest, just as if the man were not a good head taller and at least thirty pounds heavier.

At the sight of her would-be rescuer, Merry's anger melted into chuckles and she tried to keep a straight face in the blast of Zeke's indignation.

"Zeke, let me introduce Mr. William Castleton to you. He is not the one who caused the trouble. That black-cloaked loader over there. . . ." Her voice dwindled into exasperated silence for, in all the excitement, the dray, its kegs, and the two men had vanished.

Castleton gently eased Zeke back a few steps and then whispered to Meredeth, "When I saw you fall, I feared he had attacked you."

"Wal, they're gone now," Zeke muttered. "Don't do no good to shut the barn door once the cow's vamoosed. Be ya still ridin' with me, Miz Elliott?"

Quickly Merry straightened her cloak, pulled her hood up, and clutched her reticule closely to her side. "Yes, we're ready, aren't we, Anna? Anna?"

"She hit her head on that post when she jumped out of the way," Castleton advised.

In a flurry of skirts and petticoats, Meredeth rushed to kneel beside the still form. "Anna! She's unconscious. Please get me some water."

"You want I should get the doc?" Zeke offered.

"He is so busy. Could we just take her to him at the hospital? Surely there will be a spare pallet somewhere."

"Let's git her in the wagon. We kin be there in fifteen minutes," Zeke promised.

Castleton carried Anna to the wagon, where Merry padded some empty flour sacks. As soon as Zeke and Merry climbed to the seat, the vehicle rumbled away. She was surprised to see Castleton mount his Arabian and trot alongside the wagon.

"You do take your rescue work seriously, don't you?" she quipped as they pulled up in front of the red brick hospital.

"I thought you might need help getting her in," Castleton answered.

His reason was valid. Chagrined, Merry lowered her eyes and spoke softly. "I'm sorry. My sarcasm was uncalled for. You have been a great help. I do appreciate your time and effort on our behalf."

His eyes shone with humor again. "Very prettily said. You are most welcome. Come, let's be friends. You lead the way and I'll carry your maid."

It did not take them long to find Dr. Elliott. At his daughter's greeting, he came toward his visitors, a smile on his face.

"Merry, I didn't know you were coming today. Why, 'tis Anna. What happened?"

"She's unconscious, Papa. Could you take a look at her?"

"Of course. Bring her back to my examining table, please."

When Dr. Elliott discovered the lump over the maid's ear, he looked up at Merry. "How did she hit her head?"

"She slipped and fell into a post near the inn. Will she be all right?"

"Oh, Anna is a strong country girl. I'm sure she will recover. I have never known her to be clumsy before."

"She tried to protect me. We were waiting on the dock while Zeke loaded his wagon. A keg fell from a dray nearby. Anna pushed me out of the way, then she jumped aside, but she lost her footing on the wet dock. Fortunately the keg didn't hit us."

"It's a good thing she saw it in time to avoid it," Dr. Elliott said as he held the lamp closer to check Anna's eyes. The maid moved her head and groaned.

"She'll come around any time now. If there is no problem with her vision or balance, a few days' rest should do the trick. You'd best leave her here with me. I'll keep an eye on her."

Dr. Elliott suddenly realized another figure stood behind

Merry. "You have a young man with you. I don't believe we have met."

"Oh. . .yes. He was at the inn and offered his help. Papa, this is William Castleton. Mr. Castleton, my father, Dr. Lawrence Elliott."

Both men nodded tentatively.

"While I was exercising Othello yesterday, I met Mr. Castleton. He is visiting the Morelands. I believe he said it was a house party?"

At the words "house party," Dr. Elliott's eyebrows furrowed in a frown, but his innate good manners urged him to shake the man's hand.

Castleton explained, "The Morelands are cousins of my mother's. I had been visiting relatives in Virginia when I met Trevor Moreland."

"You are not from this part of the country then?"

"No. My home is in England. An uncle in Boston offered me a partnership in his shipping line. For the last few years I have been living there, though responsibilities often call me elsewhere."

Even though Castleton had resided in Boston for several years, both the doctor and his daughter stiffened when he called England his home. As if he felt the icy edges of that wall of distrust between them, the young man bowed and turned away.

"Thank you," Merry called after him.

"I hope to see you again, Miss Elliott, Dr. Elliott. I pray your maid will recover quickly. Good day."

For just a moment, blue eyes met her green ones. Then he was gone and she jerked her attention back to Anna. It would be far too dangerous for all of them to think of friendship with that young man.

When the door closed behind the Englishman, Dr. Elliott drew Meredeth into the small room he used as his own.

"That was a very personable young man, my dear. I think caution will be wise. He is British and the Morelands are trying to ride the fence between Tories and Patriots. Think carefully what you say about Matt when Castleton is around."

"Papa, I am not a child. I can guard my tongue."

"Now don't get your back up. I meant that only as a reminder. You are a young lady now and he is—"

"A very personable young man. Yes, Papa, but I love Matt too well to give him away, especially to a stranger from that country. Most likely I will see little of him. He is too busy being introduced to Tory society."

"I know you would do nothing to harm Matt. Forgive an old man his concern."

"Don't ever stop being concerned for us, Papa. Knowing you are gives us hope and courage."

Kissing him on the cheek, she made her farewells. When she closed the hospital door behind her, the smiling face of the waiting Englishman stopped her midstride.

"Could I escort you to your destination, Miss Elliott?"

"Oh. Oh no, thank you. It is not far from here and the streets are busy with townspeople. I may even see some friends on the way."

The smile disappeared from his face. She reminded herself he was not quite a friend. Still, a small portion of her heart questioned that assumption. With a brief nod, he accepted her dismissal and walked away.

Merry suddenly remembered she must catch Jim Hanks and so she quickened her steps in the direction of City Tavern. When she arrived, she found that the lunchroom was crowded, for this was one place in Philadelphia where travelers could be assured of a good meal. Locals thronged there for its fried chicken and meat pies. Merry had never seen Jim Hanks, but was sure that Molly, one of the serving girls, would know him if he were a regular customer. Molly, carrying a large tray, smiled as she hurried by.

"I jus' cleaned off a small table over there." Molly nodded direction.

Merry sat and removed her cloak. The serving girl soon

returned for her order.

"Haven't seen you for a while. I heard yur pa was busy at the hospital. Are you visitin' today?"

"Aunt Mina and I came in to shop. We have been home-bodies since Matt and Papa left. How are you doing, Molly?"

"Oh, things are quiet here, with all the young men off fightin'. I hope this war gits over soon or I'll be an old maid afore I have a steady gentleman. Whatcha want?"

"Could you make me two meat pies with ham and sauer-kraut? Papa is partial to ham and I know he's not eating as he should."

"It'll be ready quicker'n a cat can lick its whiskers."

"Before you go, Molly, has Jim Hanks been in today?"

"No–o. I don't rightly recall seein' him."

"If he comes while I'm here, will you point him out to me, please?"

"Oh, Miz Elliott, you don't wanta go anywhere with him. He's jus' sorta lazy, good-for-nothin'. There's plenty gents be callin' on you when the war's over."

"I don't want him for that kind of friend, Molly. I just want to talk to him about Matt."

"Oh, that's all right I s'pose. Well I'll git those meat pies."

Merry sat quietly, intrigued by the variety of patrons. A rather rowdy group of young men entered and took posses-sion of one of the larger tables. They had barely made them-selves comfortable before another person joined them. It was Castleton! Had they moved the house party here?

"Miz Elliott," Molly said.

Meredeth looked up just as Molly leaned closer to whisper in her ear. "That's Jim Hanks, the one with the red hair."

"Thank you, Molly. Could you ask him to come over here, please? I'd rather talk to him alone."

"All right, Miz Elliott, if you want me to."

Molly's heels clicked briskly across the floor. Clearing her throat loudly, she leaned over to speak to the red-headed man. Grinning, he looked up at the serving girl then stretched to see around her. For a full minute he stared at the quiet, auburn-haired woman across the room. Merry sat in strained silence, then lowered her eyes. Jim made some remark to his comrades that produced a wave of hilarity.

Pushing back his chair, he rose and ambled over to plant big hands on Merry's table. His brown eyes smiled just ten inches from her reddening face as he said, "I hear you're anxious to talk with me?"

Hardly knowing how to respond, Meredeth reached into her reticule and, with trembling fingers, she pushed the linen squares across the table to him. "My brother, Matt Elliott, sent these to me in a letter. Will you please be sure that either Major John Clark or Captain Charles Craig receives them immediately?"

"Matt? Are you his sister?" Then, at her stiff nod, the man's stance altered abruptly. "Thank you, ma'am. My horse is just outside. I'll see that Craig gets them as soon as I can find him."

The indolent slouch turned and, with three big strides, he returned to his table, issued a sharp command, then walked to the door. The remaining men at the table leaned heads together in earnest conversation, then exited the lunchroom with their voices raised in amiable joking.

The other customers continued to talk and eat as if nothing had happened. When Molly brought the meat pies, Merry paid for them and forced herself to walk from the restaurant at a normal gait, even though she felt like running.

two

Once outside the tavern, Merry glanced around. There was no sign of Jim Hanks's friends, and she swiftly made her way back to the hospital. When she arrived, her father was busy with a patient. Hesitant to disturb him, she smiled at the helper and pointed to the food. When the woman nodded her understanding, Merry left. Her walk to Conners Inn seemed long. She felt a sudden chill as the sun hid behind dark clouds and the wind increased.

That evening, Philadelphia's population huddled in homes, making plans. At the inn there was a great deal of commotion, and Aunt Mina insisted upon leaving immediately for Elverson. Merry shook her head sadly for the sound of artillery fire could be heard already and she knew they would not make it. The British had surely taken Chadd's Ford and possibly they were as far as Germantown. It would be much safer to remain in Philadelphia.

Kneeling beside the window, Merry wearily closed her eyes and prayed. "Heavenly Father, we are all so afraid. We've heard so many stories about the British troops in Boston. Please keep us all safe. If Matt still lives, bless him and help him. Show us what You would have us do and. . .oh Lord, please be with Papa. Send someone to help him with all the injured and, dear God, help the wounded Patriots, too. Amen."

That night Meredeth tossed fretfully on her bed, going over and over the day's events. Had she done the right thing?

Conners was a close friend of Papa's and a well-known Patriot. She hoped Jim Hanks was all that Conners believed him to be for he certainly was not what she had expected. Then there was Castleton. Why did he run with that group? Was he a spy, an English spy?

By morning, many had packed all the goods they could manage into wagons or carriages, and the road to Morrisville and Trenton was choked with traffic. Bulletins were nailed to trees, informing folks that Benjamin Franklin had sailed for France to enlist aid from friends there.

Merry tried to block out the noise and chill. She pictured them back at Cresswick, with Papa reading the Bible each morn before the fire and Mama telling them stories of great men and women of God. How she wished they had Elijah's army of angels in Philadelphia to defend them now!

≈

All that week the sounds of warfare punctuated every sentence and sent shivers of warning to the entire population. Clark's spy network kept the leaders informed of Howe's every move, and trickles of news leaked down to ordinary citizens. At the inn, Conners proclaimed his favorite topic tonight. Merry wondered if he had more information than most or if he simply talked more convincingly.

"Yessir, that Washington's a smart man. Those Brits had a right-knowing spy system. Washington and his men were bumfuzzled at first, but then he called John Craig to 'im. Now thet's one canny major. He's done set up a reg'lar comp'ney of spies. Nobody but Craig knows 'em all. He keeps 'em moving round so's nobody kin guess where they'll be two days runnin'. Like a chess player, he moves 'em. You jus' wait. He'll let tha Brits git so fur an' then he'll jump."

The innkeeper clapped his big hands together, causing two-thirds of his customers to jump. Satisfied that he had made his point, he went back to puffin' his pipe. Meredeth grinned at the dead silence in the room. Conners could hold an audience enthralled just with a clap of his hands.

"Wal, jus' hope he jumps soon afore it's too late," one of the customers mumbled as he made for the door.

Silently Merry agreed with him. Certainly Washington was intelligent and Craig was known for his ability, but they were fighting the largest and oldest army in the world. The Brits called the colonists "Rebels." What would happen if the Redcoats did take Philadelphia? It was the nearest thing to a capital that the Patriots had. There were rumors claiming that the citizens of New York and Boston were little more than prisoners. The English took whatever they wanted and none dared say them nay.

By ten o'clock, most of the customers had departed for their homes. Merry climbed the stairs to her room, thinking over all that she had heard. Artillery fire began again; it seemed to be north of the city now. No doubt they were attacking Germantown. After blowing out the candle, Merry leaned on the windowsill and stared out at the blackness. A pink glow lit the northwest. In the city a low, dark fog established itself, like an omen of doom. Buildings were snared in its grip; a stifling miasma of fear filled the air.

She moved like a sleepwalker to her bed and pulled the coverlets over her ears. Just before sleep claimed her, a niggling thought teased her mind: She had not seen Castleton for three days. Before, he had followed her like a pet dog. Where was he? Busy directing Howe to Philadelphia? That night a few tears fell before she finished her prayers for Philadelphia, for the Patriots, and yes, even for Castleton. He might be the enemy, but the Bible urges folks to pray even for their enemies, doesn't it?

Though an eerie light danced on the walls, it was still dark when shouts of alarm woke her. Women and children were crying amid a storm of sounds. Stumbling to the window, she opened it and leaned out. The streets were filled with people, horses, and wagons, all desperately trying to push through the crowd. Someone banged a fist on the door of the inn. Conners's shouted question was answered by a troubled voice.

"The Brits have crossed Swedes Ford! They'll be here by sunrise! Germantown is already in their hands."

Sunrise! That was but a few hours away.

A terrified Aunt Mina charged into the room, her abigail

trailing after her like a ghost. "Oh, Meredeth! I just knew we should have gone straight to Elverson. Cousin Ferdy would have taken us in. The British are no better than scoundrels. What will become of us now?"

"We are no more at risk here than at home," Meredeth said. "Papa is here. Perhaps he will let us help with the wounded. If we just stay together, we will be in less danger. Besides, Conners is Papa's friend. He will watch out for us. We shall keep our spirits up, obey their rules, and guard our tongues."

"I do hope you are correct, Meredeth, my dear. These are such trying times, but I suppose we must learn to live through them as you say. I just know I cannot go back to sleep. My mind is in a tizzy. Perhaps if Dela reads to me, my nerves may quiet."

"An excellent idea. Dela," Merry said as she turned to the maid hovering in the doorway, "help Aunt Mina to bed. A warm cup of milk might be just the thing. I will dress and go down to see what the latest news is."

Quickly Merry donned bodice and skirt, then hurried down the stairs. The common room overflowed with townspeople.

Though Conners's voice was strong, he had difficulty speaking over the din. Merry stood back, close to the wall.

A loud clatter brought instant silence as Conners, his face red as his shirt, clambered upon a table and shouted for attention. Except for a low buzz of whispers, the startled group complied.

"Now I want tha lot of ya ta listen. Yer in no danger here. This be a respect'ble inn an' no Brits er gonna make it any different. Jus' go back ta yer beds an' try ta sleep. There's no sense in gittin' all stirred up afore tha puddin's set. We'll break our fast at six like always an' there'll be plenty ta eat. Go on now, back ta yer rooms." He climbed down from his perch mumbling, "An' tha good Lord watch o'er us."

Merry was close enough to hear the last. When Conners came past her on his way to the kitchen, she reached out and touched his arm. "Thank you, Conners. That was well done," she said.

Wearily, Meredeth retreated to their rooms. Aunt Mina and Dela were sound asleep, the book open on the bed between them. With a soft sigh, Merry crawled into her own bed.

In the morning there was no danger of oversleeping for the street below her window was noisy and full of activity. The wagons today were piled with injured British soldiers, headed for the hospital. What would they do with the Patriots who nearly filled the place yesterday? She dressed, then peeked into the other room. Aunt Mina and Dela had not awakened yet.

The common room was already crowded and most of those seated were strangers. Some wore Redcoat uniforms, but all spoke with a British slant to their words. As unobtrusively as possible, Merry made her way around the side, through the hall, and back to the kitchen. There a red-faced Conners muttered to himself as he bustled about. The entire staff, which usually ran his kitchen so effortlessly, was stalking here and there like a flock of angry chickens. There was not a smile to be seen.

Merry almost turned back to her room, but Mrs. Landers, the head cook, saw her. She motioned for Merry to sit at the long table where the kitchen help had their meals. Covering a pot she was tending, the cook sailed around the other workers and leaned over so Merry could hear her in spite of the clamor.

"It's so full out there the rats couldn't find a hole. Though, come to think of it, there's a lot of 'em sitting right there. We got flatcakes left and applesauce. Would you like some?"

"That sounds wonderful. Yes, thank you. Are those all British out there?"

"You'd think they owned the place. Mr. Conners had a time saving your rooms for you. If more of them officers come, I don't know if he ken. You might want to keep an eye out for another place to stay, though it beats me where you could go.

Those evil men are taking over all the nice homes and either putting folks out or making them move into a back room or two while the Brits claim the best parts. They're almighty high in the instep an' that's a fact."

"Perhaps we will have to return to Cresswick."

"You won't be going anywhere but what they tell you. They got troops all around the city. Won't let none out atal."

"But where can we go then?"

"They already claimed your pa's room. Mr. Conners done took all the doc's things and stored 'em in a cubby. Mebbe you ken take 'em to him in case he has need of 'em. Have you any kin here in the city?"

"There are some friends, but I suspect their homes have been confiscated, too."

"If you cain't find a place, you let me know. Mebbe I ken help you. I'll keep me thinkin' box on it."

Mrs. Landers produced butter, a bowl of applesauce, and utensils. She maneuvered between workers to the fireplace and returned with a platter of flatcakes.

"They're nice and warm yet. Now you jus' eat up while I get the rats some cheese. Whoever heard of cheese on flatcakes! Tis disgusting." With a shake of her gray head, the cook went back to her duties.

Amid all the uproar, Meredeth asked the blessing quietly. Fear floated through that room like fog on water. When she finished, she caught Mrs. Landers's attention.

"May I take the rest up to Aunt Mina and her maid? They should be awake by now."

"Here, let me get a tray for you. Ken you carry it all right or should I send a potboy up with it?"

"I can manage, thank you. That was delicious."

Merry started toward the stairs; she shivered when a rough hand stopped her.

"Here now, missy. Haven't seen the likes of you serving before. Where have you been hiding?"

Standing as tall as her five feet, two inches allowed,

Meredeth tilted her chin and forced herself to calmness. "I am not a servant. I am a guest here. Now please have the goodness to let me pass."

"Well now, don't be so high and mighty, missy. A pretty young thing like you shouldn't be wandering around alone. Don't know what kinds of villains you might meet up with. Now I'll just escort you to your room to be sure you get there all safe and sound like, hmmm?"

"I am perfectly capable of making it to my room without help, thank you. Please remove your hand from my arm."

"You don't want to be so hard to get along with. I have authority to guarantee you'll be treated like royalty while we are here."

"The lady already has an escort, Hastings," a voice interrupted. "Sorry. I saw her first. We have become well acquainted this past week."

With one hand on the tray and the other around Merry, Castleton faced down the Redcoat officer. With sputtered anger, Hastings backed off and said nothing more, but his snapping black eyes followed them as they walked to the stairs.

"I must admit you are very good at your specialty, Mr. Castleton. Thank you again," Merry said softly.

"My name is William, but most of my friends call me Will. Surely my adroit rescue of a lovely maiden should prompt her to consider me a friend?"

Soberly, Meredeth searched his face. The congenial smile, the humorous twinkle in his blue eyes, the boyish lock of hair that seemed to have a mind of its own, and the firm but gentle hold on her arm all encouraged her to accept him for what he claimed to be. After all, she did not know for sure that he was a spy. That was only a figment of her imagination. Perhaps he helped the Patriots just as he helped her. She certainly needed a friend right now.

"Very well, we will be friends then. You can call me Meredeth if it pleases you."

"I've heard them call you Merry. I like that much better."

A teasing sparkle lit her eyes as she said, "Let us test your mettle, sir. If you can manage that tray up the stairs to our rooms without spilling anything, you may call me Merry."

The warmth of his answering grin touched her as she led the way up the steps. At the landing, a clatter behind her made Merry turn. She glanced down, following his gaze, and abruptly she lowered her skirts. Better she should fall on the stairs than have Aunt Mina chide her for showing her ankles.

Will looked up with no repentance whatsoever in his smiling features. "Those dainty feet were made for dancing."

With a huff over her shoulder, Merry hurried to the door and held out her hands for the tray. Before she could close the door on him, Will dug into a pocket and handed her a piece of paper.

"If I don't happen to be around when you need me, my helpful service is still at your command. Just send a message to this address. I mean that very seriously," he spoke low but firmly.

"Thank you Mr. . .ah, Will."

When Merry entered the room, Aunt Mina and Dela were dressed, ready to descend to the common room.

"I think you might be much more comfortable eating up here. The dining area is filled with Brits. Mrs. Landers sent up some delicious flatcakes."

"Humph! I suppose we are expected to remain secluded while those atrocious Englishmen are in charge. Well, let's see what the cook has provided. This will doubtless be our lot for some time," Aunt Mina complained.

"Mrs. Landers suggested we seek other quarters for our rooms here will soon be confiscated. Do you know of anyone who might take us in, Aunt Mina?"

Her brow furrowed in concentration, the older woman commenced to deplete the flatcakes swiftly. At last she sat back and gently patted her mouth with a napkin.

"There is an old acquaintance of mine. Her name is Elvira

Clairmont. I haven't seen her in years, but she lived in an older place on the north side. I believe it was on Arch Street. She is a widow, just a year older than I, but we grew up together as girls and attended the same schools. As I recall, she lived near Christ Church. That's about Second Street. I doubt the British would confiscate a home there. They prefer the more aristocratic places."

"If you can spare Dela, she and I can try to locate it this morning," Merry said.

Concern evident in her wide eyes, Aunt Mina nodded her agreement. "I will remain here so no one makes off with our belongings while you are gone. Such terrible times these are, when a person can be put out helter-skelter. It's shameful, that's what it is."

Swiftly donning their cloaks, Merry and Dela slipped down the back stairs to the kitchen. Conners sat, eating his own meal. The morning rush was finished and the room was much quieter.

"Mr. Conners, have you seen Jeremiah this morning?" Meredeth inquired.

" 'Tis sorry I am about the fracas this mornin', lass. This oc'apation by tha Brits ain't goin' ta be easy, that's a fact. Good thing Castleton came along when he did. That fella's right up ta snuff. Now, lessee. Jeremiah wuz here but t'wern't no place ta park tha coach. I sent him around ta tha back. Ya might just take a looksee on tha dock."

"Thank you. Oh, and Mr. Conners, Aunt Mina is staying up in our rooms while Dela and I go to speak to a friend."

"Ya best be careful now, Miz Elliott. With the whole place ov'run with Brits, there's no tellin' what could happen."

"We will be on guard. We plan to return by noon or shortly after."

Fortunately their coach was snuggled into a corner not too far away. Jeremiah left the small knot of men with whom he had been talking and hurried toward Merry.

"Can you take us to Christ Church, Jeremiah? We must

find some other place to stay."

"I kin take ya there, but then I gotta git this load ta the Brits quick like. They're making use of everything on wheels, Cain't take the chance o' gitting their dander up."

"Of course, Jeremiah. It's not your fault. They've taken over everything. Aunt Mina wasn't sure of the address, anyway. We will stop to ask the Reverend Harrison at Christ Church when we get to the neighborhood."

Everywhere they looked, the city was cloaked in subdued conversation and furtive movements. Wariness weighted the air and soldiers were stopping many vehicles and pedestrians. Merry was glad when they reached the church without incident.

They bid Jeremiah farewell and approached the familiar building. Merry knocked on the heavy wooden door leading to the Reverend Harrison's study. He must have been watching from the window, for the portal opened immediately.

"Miss Elliott, what a pleasant surprise. Do come in. Please be seated, my dear, and tell me what is on your mind."

"Reverend Harrison, I am looking for an older woman by the name of Elvira Clairmont. She is a friend of my Aunt Mina's. Is she a member of your congregation?"

The preacher's eyes twinkled. "I cannot claim the lady as part of my flock, Miss Elliott. However I have heard of her." He lowered his voice to a whisper. "She is a member of another church, but the dear lady has quite a reputation. She is extremely diligent in aiding the poor and is well thought of. She is a widow and lives just down the street on Arch. I am not sure of the address, but look for a two-story, red brick home with bright blue shutters. It is very eye-catching."

Merry smiled at his colorful description and rose to leave. "Thank you, sir. We will pay her a call. We hope to see you Sunday. Surely they must allow us to attend services. Good day."

"We should all pray for good days. Things appear quite dark at present," the reverend remarked.

"You speak truly. Thank you again for your assistance."

The two women had gone only a short way down Arch before both began to chuckle. "I think it is safe to assume that we have found the lady," Merry murmured. "Undoubtedly Mrs. Clairmont is partial to blue."

"I have never seen a home with such bright colors," Dela agreed.

The walkway was bordered on both sides by a variety of plants and the wooden door boasted a large wreath of flowers in various shades of blue cloth and tied with a red bow. Merry's knock brought a tiny, white-haired woman to the door. She wore a blue, floral-print dress of an outdated style; a white lace collar framed a face that seemed to be painted on china. Somehow the dress was at peace with the fragile figure it adorned. She smiled, though breathing a bit hard from her haste to answer the door.

"Good morning, my dears. I don't believe I've had the pleasure of meeting you, but come in. Sit a spell and tell me how I may help you."

She ushered them into a cozy parlor filled with greenery. Waving a hand in the direction of some cane chairs fluffed with pillows, she seated herself and turned to Merry and Dela in eager expectation. Merry could not help responding with a smile as she and Dela sank into the cushions.

"Mrs. Clairmont?" Merry inquired.

"Yes, that is my name and who may you be, dear?"

"I am Meredeth Elliott and this is Dela, my aunt's maid. My aunt, Mina Elliott, remembers you from her early years and wondered if you were still in the vicinity. We are staying at Conners Inn and she would dearly like to visit with you and renew the friendship you shared as girls. We set out to locate you this morning while Aunt Mina waited at the inn."

"Mina Elliott? Well, I never! It has been years since I saw her and we were such close friends. How is she?"

"Except for the passing years, she is much the same girl you knew in school. She would so enjoy meeting you again.

Would it be possible for you to come to the inn or could we meet you elsewhere?"

"Why, there's no reason for that. You must come here. My cook would be pleased to show off her skills. It's so seldom we have company anymore. So you are Mina's niece. Well, child, you are a beauty if ever I saw one. It will be a delight to have you visit. My family has moved away and I see them only occasionally. Oh but," she suddenly sobered, "have those terrible invaders come to your inn yet?"

"Yes, they have. We are taking our meals in our rooms for the men at the inn are rather brash in their conduct."

"I'm sure they are. The military men are often so uncouth. Oh child, you must come stay with me. Would it be difficult to move your things? You cannot possibly stay in a public inn under these present circumstances. I will call Nell to spruce up some rooms for you."

"I know Aunt Mina would be pleased to come, but we do not want to put you to a lot of trouble."

"Why, it will be no trouble at all. It will brighten my life to have you. Mina and I could leisurely recall old times. Do say you will come. I have plenty of room and it will be such a joy for me."

The rattle of plates announced the other member of the Clairmont household. Beaming as if she had won the lottery, a well-endowed gnome of a woman entered.

"Here ya be, Miz Clairmont. Since it was close to noon, I just thought I'd make up a batch o' butterfly cakes. You like 'em so well."

With a wink in the direction of the guests, the rotund cook placed a large tray on a nearby table. Towels were whisked away to reveal plates heaped with pastries and tiny cakes. Aunt Mina would think she was in heaven here, Merry thought as she took several pieces. Dela was given her choice of the goodies, as well.

"These are almost too pretty to eat," Meredeth said. "I have never seen such before. You call them butterflies?"

That praise brought an enormous smile to the cook's face. "They are delicious. You have a rare prize in your kitchen, Mrs. Clairmont."

"Oh, forgive me. I forgot to introduce you to Mrs. Nell Schoengert. Actually she is far more than a cook. She is my closest friend. Nell, this is Miss Meredeth Elliott, the niece of a dear friend of mine, and here is Dela, her aunt's maid."

This produced a flurry of bows until the hostess leaned toward the cook and whispered loud enough to be heard at the inn. "We need some tea, dearie. Bring some freshly brewed tea, if you please."

"Oh yessum, Mrs. Clairmont. It's all made right and proper. I'll be just a minute," Mrs. Schoengert said and then away she bustled, humming to herself.

By the time Meredeth and Dela left, it was well into the afternoon. They hurried down Arch and turned on Eighth toward the hospital. Merry had to ask where her papa wanted his things sent and make him aware of their change of residence.

three

Just as Merry and Dela reached Chestnut Street, a dark buggy stopped beside them to let the heavier traffic go by. When the wagons had passed, Merry and Dela started across the street. A sharp command from the driver of the buggy, startled them and, uncertain, they halted. The driver then leaned forward and his whip lashed out to make stinging contact with the rump of the horse pulling the buggy. It snorted savagely and reared, pawing frantically at the air, and another flick of the whip sent the beast lunging toward the two women. Screams and shouts covered the thump of running hooves. Merry and Dela grabbed each other as they leaped to escape. Two figures rushed to them, lifting and rolling with them across the thoroughfare.

Meredeth, gasping for breath, pushed herself up to a sitting position as the buggy rattled off crookedly, the horse still fighting the reins. A small crowd soon surrounded the four people on the ground.

"That horse was crazed!" Meredeth exclaimed.

"No. It was the idiot driver. He lost control."

"Shouldn't a' beat at the critter like that. Bound ta spook the beast."

Strong arms turned Merry to face her rescuer, who asked, "Are you injured?"

"Mr. . .ah, Will. Imagine you turning up just when I required rescuing."

For several long moments they stared at each other while their breathing became more normal. Then with a shaky smile, he stood and held out his hand to help Merry to her feet.

"I didn't get a good look at the driver, did you?" Will asked.

"I couldn't see his face; his hands were raised in front of it.

He wore something red around his neck. I have never seen its like before."

"Something red?"

"Yes, it hung down in a V shape, not at all like a proper neckcloth."

"Did it look like a napkin folded in half?" Will asked.

"I suppose so, but who would use red napkins?"

"It sounds like a Belchior neckcloth. In England some wear them to sporting events."

Her eyes widened and a soft gasp escaped her before she covered her mouth. Somewhere else she remembered seeing another person wearing such a neckcloth.

Will started to speak, but bystanders demanded his attention. "I think we'd better get out of the way of traffic," he suggested.

Merry nodded, for the middle of the street was no place to solve mysteries. They then turned to see how Dela had fared. A man was busily brushing dust from her skirts.

"Merry," Will said, "this is my friend, Warren Trent. He is one of the best ship captains in the business. Warren, meet Miss Meredeth Elliott."

"My pleasure, Miss Elliott," Warren Trent said.

"Can we escort you? Where were you bound?" Will asked.

"We planned to stop at the hospital. The innkeeper was unable to prevent British officers from appropriating Papa's room. We wondered where he wanted his things delivered."

"You are welcome to the use of my buggy," Will offered.

"That is kind of you. If you could wait for us to ask his wishes, we would be grateful for your help."

Will glanced toward his friend. "Are you free for a time, Warren?"

"Certainly. I am not due back at the ship for hours."

"Then let's go."

When the young people started down the street, the crowd dispersed rapidly. Within minutes the four friends reached the hospital. While Merry and Dela went in to speak to her papa, the men waited outside. Warren sent Will a knowing grin.

"I was not aware you had female friends here, Will. Is she some local contact?"

Will's face tightened and his eyes narrowed to slits. "She is a lady, my friend, certainly not a mere contact. I met her purely by accident."

"Do you think it wise to start a relationship at this time?" Warren asked.

"We do not have a relationship. She is Matt Elliott's sister, but I am convinced she knows nothing of import. She has a perfectly legitimate reason for being here."

"Touché, Will. Just take care. A lot depends on us in the months ahead."

"I know our responsibilities full well. She will cause no complications."

"I have heard men say that before."

Will's glare brought a chuckle from his companion. He threw up his hands and kept his silence. When the women joined them, there was no sign of conflict, just two gentlemen discussing trivialities.

Warren was dispatched to bring the buggy from their lodgings, and Will walked back to the inn with Meredeth and Dela. Many of the officers recognized Will, greeting him jovially. Conners led them back to a pantry off the kitchen, and he handed the large bag there to Merry.

"Ev'rything from your pa's room is here," Conners said. "Twarn't much."

"I talked to my papa a few minutes ago. He has a room in the hospital where he can sleep and work. Thank you for your help."

"Ah. . .Miz Elliott. . .you didn't by chance find a place to stay yourself, did ja?"

Meredeth smiled at Conners's embarrassment.

"Yes, we did, Conners. We can move tomorrow."

"I thank'e, Miz Elliott. That there Major Hastings is a mean'un, he is. I'll have Zeke take you and yer things to the new place soon's you're ready tomorra."

"The major does seem to have a nasty streak. I'm glad we won't have to deal with him after today."

Conners chewed on his pipe and walked away muttering, "Gittin' to be a hard thing when a man cain't even run his inn without a Brit o'erseein' him."

Will's brows ridged together in a frown as he looked after Conners. Merry bit her lip. Should she warn the innkeeper to watch what he said around Castleton? But, no. She had no proof against him. After all, he had been more than helpful to her.

Mr. Trent pulled the horse to a stop in front of the inn just as Will and Meredeth emerged. After tossing the bag into the buggy, Castleton put his hands on Merry's shoulders and looked deeply into her eyes.

"Please stay in your room tonight. Conners will send food up to you. You didn't say where you are going. I would like to see you again."

"We are to stay with an old friend of Aunt Mina's, Mrs. Clairmont. She lives on Arch Street, between Fourth and Fifth. I don't think she will mind your calling on me there. Just look for the red house with all the blue trim. It stands out."

"Good. If you need help tomorrow, send a note by Conners's potboy. I may be out, but the landlady will see that I get it."

Will scanned the street. Only a handful of men strolled away to the north; there were no others in sight. Drawing Merry closer to the buggy, he raised her hand to his lips. A smile tugged at his mouth when her complexion pinkened.

"I like the way you blush. Not many young ladies are able to do that so beautifully. Instead of a fiery red, you turn a delicate pink, just like one of my mother's favorite roses."

"You are a great tease, sir," Merry admonished him.

"Merry, I am not teasing," Will said as he leaped into the buggy.

Meredeth heard Warren's laughter as they drove off, but she also heard Will's reply. "Enough, Warren. I was not teasing. If you keep this up, I may have to retire you to captain the *Katie Lou.*"

Just what was Will doing? She wished she knew. Swiftly she went into the inn.

❧

Promptly at eleven o'clock the next morning, Zeke tapped on their door. "Be ya' ready ta go, Miz Elliott?" he asked.

Meredeth opened the door and directed him to the trunks standing to one side. She, Aunt Mina, and Dela made their good-byes to Conners and climbed into Zeke's wagon. Within the hour they were shown to bedrooms on the second floor of Mrs. Clairmont's home. Aunt Mina was delighted with her room, done in blue muslin and white lace. Their hostess begged Merry's forgiveness when she led her into the next room.

"My husband, bless his soul, was not overfond of blue, so I had a few rooms done in other colors to please him. I hope this green and red room is not offensive to you."

"Not at all," Meredeth answered, biting the inside of her cheek so she would not laugh.

She fingered the beautifully made coverlet. "This is lovely. Did you make this quilt? I don't recall ever seeing this pattern."

"It is the Starfire pattern. The coverlet was a bridal gift from my mother and I have always cherished it. But I cannot understand why she made it in red and green. Perhaps she wanted to please George, my late husband. He did have a preference for those colors. There is also a smaller, matching piece to place over your knees when riding in the carriage. If you are fond of the Starfire pattern, I will look through our trunks in the attic and find the smaller piece for you. With winter coming on, you could use it in the carriage."

"Starfire. That is a perfect name. Thank you again for your warm hospitality. Conners said the British are pressing him for more rooms and that they plan to take over the inn completely."

"Tsk. Just like the lot of ruffians they are. We shall pray Ben Franklin brings us help swiftly."

"It will take time for him to make two trans-Atlantic crossings as well as to talk to his friends. I fear we will be under British rule for some time."

"Then we shall simply have to make them leave by ourselves, won't we, dear?"

A smug smile lit the determined woman's face as she stalked off down the hall. Open-mouthed, Merry stared after her. What did she suppose four women could do to defeat the British army?

Aunt Mina and Elvira, as Mrs. Clairmont preferred to be called, spent every minute reviewing the span of their lives. After a few days, Merry felt utterly useless, and she spoke to them the next morn.

"Anna surely is ready to leave the hospital by now. Papa said just the other day she was doing well. Conditions there are crowded. Do you have need of Jeremiah today, Aunt Mina?"

"No, my dear. There is no place to go since the British set such drastic rules. Redcoats control the market and evening entertainments. No one but their Tory friends dares break the curfew. Take Dela with you."

"We may go as far as the inn. I would like to speak to Conners. With troops all over the city it is difficult to walk even a few blocks without being stopped for questioning."

The older women returned to their reminiscing. Smiling, Merry climbed the stairs to find Dela busily hanging gowns she had just ironed.

"When you are finished, Dela, can you accompany me to bring Anna back to us?"

"Oh yes, Miss Elliott. I can do mending later. It will be good to have Anna with us again."

"Then I will tell Jeremiah to bring the carriage around in ten minutes. Meet me downstairs."

Merry was not chicken-hearted but she was relieved they

did not have to walk today. Normally she enjoyed exercise, but troops were everywhere. Couriers cantered past toward headquarters; soldiers stopped many pedestrians to question them. When they approached the hospital, they saw a line of injured Redcoats waiting. Would Papa have time for visitors?

Fortunately, a buggy was pulling away.

"Just sit tight, Miss Merry. We'll swing right in behind them," Jeremiah said.

That maneuver completed, the driver helped his passengers down. With concern, he saw every one of the men standing there turn, like dominoes falling, to watch the women.

"You want I should go ta tha door with ya?" he asked.

"No, thank you, Jeremiah. You stay with the carriage. I've heard the English are looking for horses to replace animals injured or lost in battle. I wouldn't put it past them to take any animal they saw standing unattended."

"Yer prob'ly right but I'll keep an eye out for ya 'til ya git inside."

The men did not leave their places but a few called out ribald comments. One young soldier glared at his comrades, then held the door open for Merry and Dela.

"Mornin' ladies. When you're finished with your business here, I'd surely be pleased to share a cup of tea with you."

His smile was genuine. Meredeth appreciated his kindness, but his red coat reminded her of Matt. Had he been killed by one of these men?

"Thank you for your help, but we have tasks we must do." They hurried in, closing the door quietly behind them. Merry raised an eyebrow at the sight of her papa's office. Books and papers lay in staggering heaps on his desk and furniture had been pushed to the center, leaving space for one pallet on each side. There was barely enough room to walk.

In the area beyond, straw carpeted the floor. Every sort of bedding formed long rows of pallets, separated by narrow walking spaces. The next chamber was the same. Finally they found her father. Anna, holding a small tray of instruments, knelt beside him while he worked on a patient's head wound.

"Ah, there we have it! You'll recover a lot faster, my friend," the doctor said, placing the bloody bullet on the tray. Standing, he wiped his hands down his white coat.

"Now, Anna, if you'll clean that out and stitch it up for me—" His mouth gaped when he noticed Meredeth, standing not five feet from him.

"Papa," she grinned up at him, "can this be the man who required two fresh coats each day when he worked in his office?"

With a laugh, he threw one arm around her, hugging her to his side. "Hush now or I'll put you to work as I did Anna. I suppose you have come to take my assistant away from me?"

His daughter scrutinized his tired eyes and the new lines in his face. In an instant her plan was changed.

"No, Papa. It looks to me as if you are working too hard. Are you getting any rest at all?"

"Oh, I spend a few hours sleeping each night."

"But that is not enough."

She saw sad agreement in his eyes. Pictures of Aunt Mina and Elvira, so happy together, flashed through her mind. There was nothing for a young lady to do at Mrs. Clairmont's.

"Papa, I did come to take Anna back to Arch Street, but if she is able to help you, she must stay here. Could I come help, also? Aunt Mina and her hostess have so much to talk about, they don't even know I'm around."

Dr. Elliott frowned.

"Papa, this is a war. So many men are hurt. You can't do everything yourself. Please let me help. . .for Matt."

His eyes filled with his love for her. He smiled and hugged her again. "You are much like your mother. Very well, we will try it, my dear. But if the men give you the least bit of trouble, you must tell me. We'll see how it goes."

"Good. Anna and I can go back to Mrs. Clairmont's at night and bring you clean clothes each morning. Papa, where do you sleep?"

"I have been sleeping in my office. There is a small dressing room down the hall where Anna sleeps. It would be better if she could sleep elsewhere."

"Agreed. Give me your soiled clothing and I will see that it is clean for tomorrow. I'll send Jeremiah back for Anna at six. Papa, can you eat with us tonight?"

Dr. Elliott slumped. Wearily he looked around at the multitude of injured men. Squaring his shoulders firmly, he replied, "Someone has to be here for them. The other doctors in town have practices of their own. Perhaps you could send me something with Jeremiah?"

At her nod, the twinkle came back in his eyes. Meredeth felt such pride in her heart for him, it brought tears very close to overflowing.

"I love you so much, Papa," she said.

"As I do you, my dear. Now off with you and see if you can find some food for me."

Merry gave him a crooked grin. She and Dela stepped carefully between the long rows of soldiers covering the floor. The line at the door was unchanged. Ducking their heads, the young women hurried to the carriage. Jeremiah leaped down from his perch to help them in.

"Jeremiah, could you stop by Conners Inn please, before we go back to Arch Street?"

"Be glad to, Miz Elliott."

When they arrived at the inn, there was no room to pull aside and wait, so after Jeremiah helped Meredeth and Dela down, he drove around to the back. At the front of the inn, Redcoats lounged about, talking in groups. Meredeth and Dela wove a path through them to the door.

A large hand on Merry's elbow made her twist away, a haughty expression tightening her face. When she saw that it was Will, a huge sigh escaped her. Delight shone in his eyes.

"I believe you are truly glad to see me. May I help you through this crowd?" Will asked.

"Yes, please. I'm afraid my five feet and two inches will

not impress any of this group and, yes, it is a relief to see you here. I'd prefer not to encounter Hastings."

Pleased with her answer, Will put a protective arm around her and motioned for Dela to stay close behind.

"Ah, Castleton is taking his little ladybird for a walk. In such close quarters, it does give one opportunity to take liberties, does it not?"

Will stopped short. Pushing Merry between himself and Dela, he turned to glare at Hastings's sneering visage. A large mug of ale was within Will's reach. His eyes intent on Hastings, Will picked up the drink as if to take a swallow, but a swift movement upturned the mug over Hastings's head. Conversation quieted. The Redcoat's guttural reply was easily heard.

"I will see you dead for this!" Hastings exclaimed.

"I will meet you any time," Will said, tossing the metal cup aside with a grimace of distaste.

Enraged, Hastings snarled, his hand dropping to his sword before he realized the impossibility of a sword fight in such a crowd. His jaw hardened and his voice dropped an octave.

"You know full well we were told not to make trouble among the populace, you swine," Hastings muttered.

"That did not occur to you when you maligned this lady. You are all mouth and no muscle. I insist you owe Miss Elliott an apology."

"Englishmen do not apologize to Rebels."

A swift movement slammed Hastings against the wall. The major's mouth gaped at the slim French dagger making a deep dent in his waistcoat. Instantly the crowd hushed, except for one rough voice that said, "Poke 'im with it, matey. Let's see if he does have blue blood as he claims."

"Apologize," Castleton growled.

Perspiration popped from the major's brow. Swiftly his eyes assessed the disgusted looks of his countrymen and the eager expectations apparent in some ragtag seamen standing at the bar. He struggled to clear his throat.

"I. . .I. . .ask your pardon," he said.

Will eased the pressure of the blade. "Get out of here before I forget who we both are."

Those around them immediately moved, making way for Hastings, who, without a backward glance, stumbled from the room.

"Aww right now, let's git back to our vi'tals. There's a flummery for dessert tonight. Got some fresh apples an it's right tasty."

Conners's suggestion brought most of the men back to the tables. Will moved his charges around the group and out to the warmth of the kitchen.

Mrs. Landers hurried to greet them and she pointed to the big table. "Thar now, jus' set you down an' I'll dish up some fried chicken an' dumplins'."

Meredeth was not sure if she wanted to thank Will or scold him for taking such a chance. As if he knew exactly what she was thinking, he leaned over to whisper.

"I knew he wouldn't fight," Will said. "Hastings talks brash, but he's a coward at heart. I carry weapons for protection, but I've never yet had to cut or shoot anyone. Christ managed without sword or gun. My tutor was a clergyman and he told me a true gentleman uses the good sense God gave him first and his fists second, if necessary. Weapons are to be used only when lives are in danger. I think he was a very wise man."

Merry's eyes misted over. "I think so, too," she murmured, "but what am I going to do with you? You always arrive just in time to rescue me, but then I never needed rescuing until I met you."

"Merry, if I could get you and your aunt out of Philadelphia, would you go?" Will asked.

She stared wide-eyed at him for a few minutes before answering, "How could you do that? Who, or what are you, Will?"

He swallowed hard as if he hadn't meant to say that at all.

Clearing his throat, he spoke more softly. "Merry, I must leave town for at least a week. If that fiend, Hastings, dares to harm you while I'm gone, I would never forgive myself. Please believe me. I'm part owner of a shipping line operating out of Boston. My home is there, but I have to travel because of business. I work hard, go to church on Sundays, I'm a gentleman and try to behave as one. . .and I like you very much. I don't want Hastings to get his dirty hands on you. Can you understand that?"

She saw truth in what he said, but there was so much he was not saying. In any event she could not leave. Her papa must remain and he needed her. She would be careful to have Dela with her at all times.

"I know there is danger for all of us, but my family is here in Philadelphia. Papa is working so hard I fear for his health. Today he agreed to let me help him. I am going to do that, Will, but I do appreciate your friendship. . .truly."

He closed his eyes and ran nervous fingers through his hair, pushing it back from his forehead.

"I should have known you'd say that. There's got to be a way. . .someone I can trust to protect you. Merry, you have no conception of the devilish things Hastings might do. All right. I do understand what you're saying, but I want you to promise me one thing."

His eyes held hers and she felt his piercing gaze all the way down to her heart. Merry licked her dry lips.

"What do you want me to promise?" she asked.

"Just that you will think carefully about any letter that comes to you that is sealed with this ring. Take a close look at it. . .memorize the pattern. Promise me that, please, Merry?"

He reached a hand to cover hers. She was struck by the force of his concern and his. . .what? What exactly was the message he was trying to convey to her?

"I will try," Merry answered. She could tell he was not satisfied with her response, but it was all she could give at this time.

Mrs. Landers plopped down a platter of chicken and a bowl of dumplings, moist with butter. One look at their sober faces made her frown. Within minutes she was back, bringing warm bread and a small bowl of peas. Hands on hips, she regarded the two young people.

"Thar's e'nugh fightin' goin' on round here without you two starting a battle. Now jus' you fill up on that and talk nice to each other, you hear? I saved this special fer you an' I don't wanta see good food go to waste." With that pronouncement, she stomped away to tend to other chores.

The somber moment broke Merry and Will into smiles, and they did justice to the delicious food before them. From the big hearth, the cook nodded wisely and set up a new batch of dough. When they were done, Will left and Merry went back to Mrs. Clairmont's.

four

The next morning when Merry awoke, a note lay beside her pillow. Startled, she picked it up. The seal of the letter had been imprinted by Will's ring. Quickly, Merry opened and read it.

> *My dear Merry,*
> *There is a soldier, Douglas McClanahan, at the hospital. He is badly injured and will be there for sometime. If for any reason you need my rescuing services, don't write a note. Just tell him. He'll contact me. I beg you to trust me.*
>
> > *Your friend,*
> > *William Castleton*
> *Please destroy this note immediately.*

Meredeth sat straight up in bed. Will was gone. Why hadn't he told her he was leaving so soon? Was it such a big secret? Don't write notes, he had said. Destroy this letter. Trust him. *Oh, Will, what are you involved with that must be hidden?*

"William Castleton, don't you dare be a British spy or I. . . I'm afraid I will be left with a totally broken heart. First Matt and now this!"

She threw the letter from her as hard as she could, but a brisk morning breeze wafted it back to the coverlet. After stretching to reclaim the bit of parchment, she jerked the Starfire quilt up over her head. Muted sobs shook the bedclothes until all her despair and frustration drained away. Only the loneliness was left. She drew in a jagged breath and whispered a prayer.

"Dear heavenly Father, thank You for Your promise that

45

You will never leave me nor forsake me. Give me the courage I need to do what I can and trust in You to watch over us. I know You can do all things. Grant me the patience to wait for Your grace to unfold Your Will. Amen."

A gentle rap at the door alerted her to the fact that the sun was well up. Dela came into the room, balancing a tray of food. The smell of honey muffins coaxed Merry from the bed's warmth, and she quickly pulled on her robe and sat cross-legged on the bed. She had plans to help her father today.

"It was getting late, Miss Merry, so Cook said to bring you a tray. Why, Miss Meredeth! Whatever made your eyes so red? Is there aught I can do?"

"Thanks, Dela, but there's nothing anyone can do. It's the way the world is. With war, occupation forces, and Papa so busy he looks sick, I guess it all overwhelmed me a bit. I'll wash my face with cold water. We should leave as soon as possible. Are Papa's clothes clean?"

"Yes, Miss Merry. They're ready. I'll lay your things out for you. Should I tell Jeremiah to bring the coach?"

"Please do. It won't take long to eat. It smells so good and I am hungry. If you will help me dress, we should be able to leave in thirty minutes. Is there a fire in the kitchen hearth, Dela?"

"That there is, Miss Merry. Cook's baking butterflies again."

"Good. You might save a few for me. Aunt Mina likes those so well they may be gone when I come home this eve."

"Yessum."

Merry rolled the note in her hand into a tiny cylinder and then she sped down the back stairs to the kitchen. Good. It was empty. Swiftly she dropped the message into the flames, staying long enough to be sure that only ashes remained.

The cool water in the basin felt good when Merry splashed it on her face and hands. The weather was warm for October, and she thought of her father in the crowded rooms of the hospital and the Patriots surrounded by smoke and heat from the big cannons. Suddenly it occurred to Meredeth that lately there had been no gunfire and that all that the townspeople heard were rumors of British victories. Were they fighting now? Where was Will? She shook that thought away and tugged on her chemise as Dela entered.

"The coachman is bringing the carriage around, Miss Merry. Here, let me help you with those buttons."

Their four hands made swift work of the task, and by the time Aunt Mina called up to inform them that the coach awaited, Merry and Dela were descending the stairs.

The heat that day was the talk of the entire city. Some said it was a belated breath of summer, others dourly whispered it was unnatural, the work of the devil, or perhaps the British. By noon, when the hospital workers stopped to eat, Merry longed for a cool bath. Perspiration ran in trickles down her back, and her hair not only rejected pins but even the riband that she tied about it.

After lunch Merry went to check on a young English soldier, little more than a child, whose fever was aflame. She hurried for more cool water for, British or not, the lad was too young to die. While she bathed his head and neck, her papa came to see the patient.

"I don't like the looks of this. His wound must be festering inside. Do you feel up to helping me or should I ask Anna?"

"Just tell me what I must do," Merry replied.

"Get the tray of instruments Anna keeps ready for me. Bring plenty of cloths and the bottle of laudanum on my desk. It's best he does not regain consciousness while I work."

Merry knelt beside the pallet, as she had seen Anna do. Dr. Elliott pierced the partially healed wound, releasing a pool of noxious ooze.

"Catch it in some cloths, Merry. I want to look at it closely when we are finished. Now pour some of that clear liquid into another cloth and hand it to me."

The boy's body jerked as her papa dipped the cloth into the

wound, swathing it clear of all infectious matter.

"Give him a bit of laudanum. You'd better hold his head so he swallows it."

Obediently Merry performed that task, then sat back on her heels as she watched her father close and bandage the shoulder again. Merry felt sure her face must be white as parchment, but she lifted a determined chin and tried to smile for her papa's benefit.

"Thank you, my dear. You are an excellent assistant, much like your mother. Now perhaps you could sit and read letters to some of the men? It will cheer them to hear from loved ones. Sometimes that is as good as any medicine I can give them."

"I don't know what they would do without you, Papa. You treat them as you would any of our men."

"Each is someone's husband or son, Merry, and I hope that Matt would receive the same care if he is ever wounded. I can do no less."

As Merry collected all the letters, she thought soberly of her feelings toward the British. Her papa was right, but it was hard to feel sorrow for them, especially since they might have killed Matt. She flicked through the correspondence.

"Douglas McClanahan," she read. "That's the name Will mentioned. I must see him next."

A craggy featured Scotsman lay staring up at the flies on the ceiling, his hands crossed over his chest, his fingers drumming that part of his anatomy as if he were playing a tune. Her approach brought a big smile to his bearded face.

"Well now, lassie, it's a sight for sore eyes to see you coming to me wi' mail in your hands. Is it a letter you bring then?"

"I do, indeed. Let me kneel here beside you so I don't disturb the others who are sleeping."

"Some sleep because they ha' no letters. 'Tis a hard thing for a mon to lay when he's used to doing a day's work. Do you write to some lad, too?"

Merry's lashes lowered and her tears trembled close to

spilling over. How she wished she could write to Matt.

"Och, forgive me, lass. I dinna mean to cause sadness for someone as bonnie as you. Have you lost a loved one then?"

She looked up, cleared her throat, and attempted a smile.

His big roughened hands gathered hers gently between his.

"Mr. McClanahan—"

"I'd be asking you to name me Red Mac, ma'am. That's how my friends call me."

Merry glanced at the brilliant shade of his hair. This time her smile was real.

"Red Mac. That's a fitting name, sir. I am Meredeth Elliott." She leaned closer to whisper. "Will Castleton told me to speak with you if I ever needed his help."

A grin divided the Scotsman's face, ear to ear. "So you are Will's lassie. The boy always did have a good eye for the bonnie ones. Did you want a message delivered?"

"Not at present. I truly came to read your letter to you unless you'd prefer to do it yourself."

"Oh, I'm right able to read, Miss Elliott. It's my legs that give me trouble, but I'd much rather listen to you. Don't think there's aught in there your ears shouldn't hear."

That earned a big smile and, with quick fingers, she broke the seal. A warm feeling flowed through her as she read of a loving family, a cottage with a glowing hearth, and freshly baked bread with molasses. When she at last folded the missive and handed it to him, she caught a hint of moisture in his eyes.

"You must miss them greatly," she said.

"Oh aye, but a soldier learns to hold his dear ones in his heart 'til he can hold them in his arms, you know. 'Tis not likely I will see them for a long while yet."

Merry surprised herself by blurting out, "I pray it will be very soon you are united with them, Red Mac."

What amazed her most was that she meant it with all her heart, and she had to admit that all Englishmen were not bounders. When she rose to leave, he grabbed her hand.

"Be sure if you need help, lass, I'll get word to Will for you. I think the lad's outdone himself this time."

"You, sir, are as big a tease as Will." With that, Merry went on to the next recipient of mail.

Somehow the rest of the day breezed by as if on wings. When Jeremiah came for the women, hovering storm clouds foretold of a noisy bit of weather ahead, but the world looked brighter in her eyes at least.

It was a wild night. Lightning flashed gaudy streaks across the sky while the accompanying thunder rattled windows in the old house. What did men in the battlefields do during a storm? Was Will on one of his ships? There were often disasters along the coast.

"Oh please, God, send Your holy angels to keep him safe."

ॐ

After the storm moved on, the temperatures cooled a bit. As the weeks passed by, each day became much like the one before as healed British soldiers were replaced by newly wounded ones. All the injured Rebels were taken to prison. Merry listened anxiously to the men's conversation, hoping for some news of the war, but they spoke only of their homes and families.

At the Mrs. Clairmont's, Elvira and Aunt Mina continued to chatter like children about the early days. Merry sighed for no one wanted to talk about the war and she longed to hear of the Patriots' progress, of their small army, and the ships at sea. Now and again, though, her papa would go to a meeting and from him she learned several things. Congress had fled to Lancaster; the State House bell, and all other bells in town, had been hidden so the English would not melt them down for cannon balls; and Washington had attacked Howe's main camp in Germantown, but had been repulsed.

One cold night Merry and Dela stayed until ten o'clock to care for the patients, while Dr. Elliott slipped away to a secret town meeting. There the populace was in an uproar for the Brits had invaded the Old Pine Church, chopped up the pews for firewood, and took the minister away for questioning. Howe was angry because the preacher had spoken strongly against the English.

"It was all a few sane citizens could do to prevent open rebellion. We'd have been shot down before we'd gone ten paces from the meeting site. The place was surrounded by Brits when it was time to leave. Fortunately the brewer had an old tunnel he used to unload kegs from the ships and store them in a small cave under his property. We all escaped undetected," Dr. Elliott whispered as Merry donned her cloak to leave.

"Oh, Papa, please be careful," she implored.

"I will, my dear. We can change our meeting place. John Craig is searching for the informant. Let me see if Jeremiah is waiting."

He glanced outside, then nodded to Merry. "You go right to Mrs. Clairmont's now. If anyone stops you, tell them you worked late at the hospital. Most of the men know you help me and they will not cause trouble."

After a last hug, Merry and Dela ran swiftly to the vehicle, and within minutes of reaching Arch Street, they hurried in silence to their rooms. Merry leaned against the closed door; an icy shiver shook her. What sort of men would damage a beloved landmark? A church!

"I wonder what the minister said that put them into such a fury? How I wish I could have heard him."

The water in the basin was cool, but it felt good against her skin heated by the anger building up inside. She pulled on her gown, climbed into the big bed, and went to sleep.

When she awakened, the air was much cooler and it was still dark out. A scrabbling noise outside brought her fully alert. Did Mrs. Clairmont have a cat? Perhaps a wild animal was looking for something to eat. Curious, she tugged on her robe and hurried to open the window, where a fist-sized rock lay on the sill. From the yard below, a sudden movement made Merry turn. Was that the tail of a cloak whipping around the gate? She could not tell for bushes hid the answer. Her gaze again centered on the rock and she realized that someone must have placed it there by climbing up one of the nearby maples thrashing a macabre dance and beating time on the house.

Merry stepped away, her back to the wall, until her hand touched the bed. A tug drew the Starfire quilt closer to her and she wrapped it around her shoulders like an overly large cloak. Bone-chilling shivers shook her slender form and shallow gulps of air only made her colder, but the approaching dawn lent enough vague light to assure her that the room was now empty, except for the simple furnishings.

Aftershock turned her limbs to jelly and she sat on the bed, her head in her hands. Who would do such a thing? The rock! There was parchment tied to it. Merry hurried to the window, knowing that she would simply read the note and all would be explained.

It took a disgusting amount of time to untie the string and free the parchment. Merry then fumbled for taper and flint and, after several strikes, it was lit. Squinting in the meager glow of candlelight, she stumbled over the water-soaked words.

> *D r M ry,*
> *T is mus re h ohn Cra im edi ly.*

The second page was a jumble of letters and numbers. The outer sheet had protected them fairly well.

"Evidently it is intended for John Craig, but who could have sent it? It's not Matt's handwriting. Oh, it just doesn't make sense," Merry muttered to herself. In her heart she knew it had to be code.

"I'll have to take the morning off at the hospital and get this to Jim Hanks. I wonder if the British have taken over City Tavern, too?"

Dela tapped at the door, then entered with a bowl of apple-sauce pudding and morning chocolate. Swiftly Merry hid the rock and note among the covers. Only after she was fully dressed did she place the parchment in a pocket of her petticoat.

When Jeremiah helped her into the carriage, she asked, "Could you wait for me this morn? After I see Papa, I must go to City Tavern."

"Of course, Miz Elliott. I ken wait and take you back to the hospital, too."

"That won't be necessary. I don't know how long it will be. I will take Dela with me."

The coachman nodded agreement, but later, when he noted the groups of Redcoats inside, he spoke up. "Miz Meredeth, it jus' ain't proper to leave you like this an' you know it."

"I can't keep you waiting all day for me, Jeremiah. You know full well Aunt Mina and Mrs. Clairmont will need the coach today. It's market day."

The faithful Jeremiah scowled but could not argue with the truth. He reluctantly pulled away.

As they entered, Merry whispered to Dela, "Look for a table in the corner near the kitchen door. Molly will keep an eye out for us. She is a good friend."

The luncheon crowd had not yet arrived. Two waitresses were busily serving the Redcoats. After a lengthy wait, a younger girl came to take the women's order.

"We got no ham today, nor taters, either. Ma says you can have fried chicken or clam chowder. We got plenty biscuits."

"Is Molly here today?" Merry asked with a smile.

"No'um. She done took sick an' went home yeste'day."

Merry's hopes disintegrated. She feared Jim Hanks might not come since the Brits had discovered the source of good food here. She had seen no sign of the tall redhead.

The child misunderstood their silence. Eagerly she added, "I can bring ya' milk with tha' biscuits. Ma jus' took 'em from the oven. She says long as we got chickens, an' the cow don't go dry, we'll have somethin' at least. Can't hardly get beef or ham no more."

"Milk and biscuits sound very good," Merry said, her eyes twinkling at the child's gamin grin as she marched off.

"They've been having trouble getting supplies for the hospital, too. Papa is discouraged about it because he can't get some of the medicines he needs. You'd think it was to their advantage to provide medicines for their own troops," Merry told Dela.

"Here ya' be, ma'am, nice and hot from the hearth fire." The child placed two brimming mugs of milk plus a mound of fragrant biscuits in front of them.

"That smells delicious. What is your name, please?" Merry asked.

"I be Jesse, ma'am."

"Well, Jesse, we thank you for your help. I didn't know there was such a scarcity of food in town."

"The Brits take ev'rything. Don't know what we'll do for next week. Jim Hanks done promised he'd bring us some if he can."

"You know Jim Hanks, Jesse?"

"Yessum. He's my cousin."

Merry's heart did a flip-flop. Could she find a way to reach Jim without entering City Tavern? She felt so vulnerable sitting here.

"Jesse, is there a table in the kitchen where Dela and I can eat? The Redcoats stare at us here."

"Ma said she worried 'bout you. She'd not fuss if you came back there. I can help carry the plates."

Within minutes they were seated at a long table used by the help. Mrs. Wilkins welcomed them; a few minutes of conversation made clear her feelings toward the Englishmen.

"Does Jim Hanks still come in regularly?" Merry ventured.

"He takes his lunch back here. He's a good boy. We'd pro'bly be out of food by now without him."

"Mrs. Wilkins, is there some way I could get a message to him?"

"I'd be glad to give him your message, ma'am," the cook promptly replied.

"Oh, I do thank you, Mrs. Wilkins."

Lifting her skirts, Meredeth removed the folded note from her petticoat pocket and handed it to the cook. With a wink, Mrs. Wilkins shoved it into her bodice and quickly smoothed the material over it.

The door to the kitchen banged open. A red-coated officer stood glaring at them. It was Hastings!

"Just what is going on here?" Hastings demanded. "We ordered some of your biscuits at least a quarter-hour since. I see you serve Rebels before us. Just remember who the majority of your customers will be from now on, Mrs. Wilkins. Henceforth you will serve us immediately and respectfully or this place will be closed!"

five

Major Hastings stomped out the door, slamming it behind him like a petulant child.

"That's Hastings, Howe's right-hand man. He's got a mean temper, he has. Why don't you two jus' leave by the back door? No sense in you havin' to walk back through there."

With a last thank-you, Merry and Dela left and started for the hospital. They had gone only a few feet when an unfamiliar voice stopped them.

"Miss Elliott, is it not?" the voice asked.

Merry jerked around to face a pleasant smile above a red coat. "Y–yes, I am Miss Elliott."

"I saw you at the hospital the other day. I'm going there. Would you object to my walking with you?"

"Why no, certainly not, sir. I would welcome your company. It is not easy for a lady to walk these streets now, even though her abigail is with her."

She managed a smile and motioned for Dela to follow; her mind racing, she tried to behave normally. Had Hastings sent this man to check on her? He appeared to be very congenial, but an apprehensive shiver flickered through her. Merry took a deep breath; she could act a part as well as the next one. Perhaps his presence would prevent them from being accosted by others. He was an officer, after all.

"Permit me to present myself," he said. "I know under other circumstances I should wait for another to introduce us, but the conditions make that unlikely. I am Major Henry Stanfield and you are. . .?"

"Miss Meredeth Elliott. My papa is the doctor at the hospital on Spruce. Because of the extra burden of patients, I am helping him." That should sound friendly enough and quench

56

any doubts he had about her.

"What a diligent young lady you are. You remind me much of my sister. That's why I wanted to speak with you. Truth to tell, all my friends will be jealous, I assure you, to see me walking with such a lovely lady."

Merry ducked her head. *Flattery will not go far with me,* she thought, *especially from an Englishman.*

"I'm from Hambledon in Hampshire, England, a sleepy little town. Philadelphia is larger, but its countryside is similar. Have you always lived here, Miss Elliott?"

"We live west of here. My aunt and I were visiting and shopping when your troops took Philadelphia. Now we must remain."

"Then I am doubly fortunate in meeting you. I realize this is most hasty, but would you object to attending a ball with me this Friday eve? When we see your father, I would be pleased to show him my credentials. There will be other young ladies from town there."

"A ball? In the midst of a war?"

"Perhaps it seems callous, Miss Elliott. Yet we men must have some recreation. Do at least consider my invitation. It is lonely for those of us who have no kin in this area."

Merry looked up at the young man beside her who was as tall as Will. He sounded sincere, but a true Patriot should not attend a ball with a Redcoat officer! "You must see the position into which I would be placed. I understand that you could be lonely, so far from home. Yet I must refuse your offer."

"Please think on it. I would like to know you better. I'm a gentleman of very good background, truly."

He said no more until they reached the red brick hospital. When he accompanied her through the entrance, she glanced up at him.

"At least let me come in and meet your father," he requested. "I have heard much good of him."

"Of course. I will introduce you and then I must attend to my duties."

When they found Dr. Elliott, he was about to set a broken leg and Anna stood ready to help. Dr. Elliott noticed Merry and then began to give brisk orders.

"Anna, hold his left arm. Merry, take his right. Your friend can anchor the right leg, if you will, sir?"

The startled expression on Stanfield's face changed to one of understanding and, with a nod, he stepped forward and grasped the soldier's leg. Merry brimmed with pride as her papa worked carefully to ease the disconnected bone into place. When the wound was clean and bandaged, Dr. Elliott looked up.

The Englishman extended his hand with a smile. "Well done, Doctor. I've heard of your excellent reputation but never dreamed I'd be able to participate in your work. Thank you for allowing me that experience. I'm Major Stanfield, sir. I just had the pleasure of meeting your lovely daughter and escorting her here."

"Then I am in your debt. Do you have a friend in the hospital?"

"Yes I do, but I fear that was not my reason for coming today. I was attempting to coax your daughter to attend a local ball with me. Before you say yea or nay, sir, may I present my credentials to you?"

His daughter's low sound of distress was not lost on Dr. Elliott and he raised a warning eyebrow. Patiently he read the papers given him, then handed them back.

"My lord, I am sure you are all you claim to be. I have no objection to your taking Meredeth to a ball for she has had little enough enjoyment lately. Yet she is of age to decide for herself and I have respect for her judgment."

"But, Papa—"

"Meredeth, I know of the major from others. He is a gentleman and a scholar." The doctor's eyes twinkled as he continued. "He is also a friend of Benjamin Franklin. Is that not true, sir?"

Merry stiffened. For some reason, Papa wanted her to accept this man's invitation. But why, when their countries were at war? She looked up to deep blue eyes and a boyish smile. Oh well, if Will could dance at balls during a war, so could she!

"Major Stanfield, I thank you for asking me to attend this party with you. If you promise to tell me of your knowledge of Benjamin Franklin, I accept."

He could not be all bad. The eager look of delight was surely real. He caught her hand in his and raised it to his lips.

"Thank you, m'lady. I look forward to it. The ball will be held at the Nicholas Curry home. I'll pick you up in my carriage at eight, Friday next. Now, if you will excuse me, I must go." As he exited the hospital, there was a jaunty step to his gait.

Merry turned a calculating gaze to her papa. "Now, Papa, what was that all about?"

"It can do no harm for you to be seen with him, my dear. His escort will insure your safety. He appears an agreeable chap and. . ."

"And what, Papa?"

"You need some frivolous pleasure in your life, and I think you could have no better friend among the British."

"Oh, Papa! Very well, I will go with this paragon."

୬

In her room that evening, Merry held up one of the gowns she had with her. Yes, it would do for the ball. Humming a melody, she circled the room, imagining herself waltzing at the ball. Somehow Will's face replaced Stanfield's in her mind's eye and the room suddenly felt warm. She put aside the gown and moved to the window. Raising the sash, Merry leaned into the welcome breeze. The trees waved in a waltz of their own.

Just then she noticed a cloaked form scurry from a shrub to the tree! Her first reaction was to close the window and move to one side, but a small, rotund person slipped out to meet the intruder. For mere seconds they made one misshapen shadow, and then the short figure returned to the kitchen. Suddenly, Merry shrank back, for the cloaked stranger was climbing the tree outside her window!

Quickly she ducked behind the curtains in the corner where her clothing hung. He was almost to the windowsill! Then his hand reached out and, with a mighty leap, he dropped from sight.

Merry's shaking fingers flung open the curtains behind which she had hidden. It took no more than a second for her to reach the window. He was gone! Gathering the rags of her courage about her, she lit a candle, picked up the rock, and removed the note.

> *My thanks for the quick delivery last time. This must go the same route. Take care what you say at Nicholas Curry's ball.*

Merry fell back on the bed, her mind awhirl. How could the sender of these notes know she was going to the ball? She only learned of it herself late today. Somehow she must find time to deliver the message. Would she ever know the mysterious stranger's identity?

❧

The next morning when Merry stopped in the kitchen to ask Nell to pack a lunch for them, she watched the cook carefully. It must have been Nell in the garden, for Mrs. Clairmont was far too slim. Later that day the message was duly delivered to Mrs. Wilkins. She and Jesse appeared pleased to be taking part in the subterfuge.

That week there was no word from Jim Hanks, and Merry alternated between excitement and concern. The night of the ball her eyes sparked with anticipation as she twirled before the oval mirror in Aunt Mina's room.

Mrs. Clairmont called up the stairs, "You have a gentleman caller, Meredeth."

Merry caught up her shawl and reticule, then walked sedately down the stairway. The major stood there at the bottom of the steps, awaiting her. From the expression on his face, he was well pleased with what he saw.

"Lovely lady, I shall be the envy of all my colleagues," he said softly as he bowed before her.

Aunt Mina was right behind her. "Mind you now, Meredeth must be home by one of the clock," she informed them.

Stanfield smiled indulgently. "I have given my word, ma'am. Be at ease."

When the major's carriage pulled up before Nicholas Curry's home, a warm welcome awaited them. The ballroom shimmered with gaily swinging skirts and red uniforms twirling about to the music. A great many eyes inspected Stanfield's partner. Meredeth was introduced to several of the major's close friends, then whisked away as a new set formed.

"I believe ladies are allowed to give their escort two dances and the supper dance in your society. Is that correct?" he asked as they followed the pattern of the steps.

"That is true in most cases, but I have no dance card yet," Merry reminded him.

"Then we will acquire one before I relinquish you to the others. You are by far the most beautiful lady in attendance. I refuse to give my partner up except when absolutely necessary. Will you save your waltzes for me?"

Merry teasingly glanced up through her lashes. He was a marvelous dancer and all she could ask for in a partner. His charm seemed genuine and, whatever his motive, she was having a delightful time.

"I will save two for you, Major Stanfield. Thank you for bringing me. I have missed dancing and parties."

He twirled her through the final steps, leaving her breathless. When he bowed over her hand, Merry could feel others crowding around them. Before she could be seated, three young men bowed before her. Two had big smiles and shining eyes. The third was very angry! Merry's mouth flew open and she backed a few steps.

"Sorry, friends. This dance is mine." Castleton clamped one large hand over her small one and pulled her toward the set that was forming.

"Will, whatever is the matter?" she whispered to his back.

Without a word he whirled her into place and took his stance opposite her. His almost-smile was grotesque and his eyes glared as if she had trounced on his foot.

"Will. . ." she began, and then the music sent the couples dipping and turning and it was impossible to carry on a conversation.

"What are you doing here?" he muttered when they had a few steps together.

"I was invited," she retorted before they moved apart.

"Who?" was all he had time for at the next meeting.

"Stanfield," she sputtered angrily back at him.

Who did he think he was that he might dictate where she went and with whom? She thought they were friends, but she did not need a papa. She had a very good one.

His eyes were softer when he put his arm around her waist for the final promenade under raised hands of the other dancers. He leaned close to whisper.

"Don't you realize this is dangerous for you, Merry?"

"Dangerous? Why? Papa thought it was a good idea."

"But he doesn't know all the facets of it. Don't mention Matt, whatever you do. Promise?"

With a quizzical expression, she examined the worry in his eyes. "I won't, unless someone asks if I have a brother. Then I will only give his name. How do you know Matt?"

There was no time for him to answer for she was deluged with requests for dances. Stanfield shouldered through the press of admirers to hand her a dance card. No sooner had he given it to her than Will's big hand took it away. Only after filling in three dances did he return it to her. Before others claimed the card, she was able to glance at it. Stanfield, true to his word, had marked his name on two waltzes and the supper dance; Will had taken the other two waltzes and a promenade.

In a daze, she managed a smile for the young officer who claimed the next dance. Her mind and heart were both behaving badly. The first was confused, the second was both pleased and worried. She smiled, bowed, and dipped in time to the music, but her thoughts danced to a wilder step. Why was Will so angry at first? How much did he know about Matt? He wasted no time in coming to the dance. Yet he hadn't let her know he was in town. When Will bowed to take her off to the next waltz, she had come to no conclusions.

They said nothing at first, but his hand held hers tightly. She felt his chin brush the top of her head when they twirled, and he clutched her as if he feared she might spin off on one of the turns.

"I am glad you are back in town. Will you be able to stay awhile now?" she ventured.

"I have a ten-day here before my next ship sails. I know you help your father, but when can I see you?"

"We come home at six each evening. I'm sure Mrs. Clairmont would be happy to have you call."

"How about tomorrow and Sunday?"

"It is the same on Saturdays. Sundays we all attend church and rest. I just wish Papa could do the same. He is so tired."

"I'll be at Mrs. Clairmont's at seven tomorrow eve. Is that agreeable?"

"We will be glad to receive you then. Will, why were you so angry when you first saw me tonight?"

He pulled her a bit closer, then relaxed. "I suppose it was the shock of seeing you with a Redcoat. Oh, Merry! I wanted to take you to dances and parties and I have not been able to do that. You are a very special person to me. I want to know you better, much better. Also I worry about Hastings hurting you in some way. He can be a terrible beast when angered."

For a moment they simply stood, staring into each other's eyes and hearts. Then a chuckle nearby awoke them to the fact that the music had stopped and the dance floor was clear. Will's head jerked up to find another Redcoat waiting very patiently for the next dance. Gruffly, Will tried to smile at the man as he handed Merry over to him.

six

Promptly at seven, Will's buggy stopped in front of the Clairmont home; he covered the space from there to the house in giant strides. Nell Schoengert opened the door and directed him to the parlor, where Mrs. Clairmont smiled a welcome.

"Do come in, young man, and be comfortable. We are enjoying evening tea and cakes."

Merry introduced him to their hostess and her aunt. Will bowed to the older women before he allowed his gaze to stray toward Merry. Elvira poured each a cup of tea, while Nell offered plates of butterflies and lemon tarts.

"Have you ever tried these, Will?" Meredeth asked.

She was happily devouring a confection in the shape of a butterfly and held a half cup of tea. Obviously he couldn't carry her away immediately, so he sat down and reached for a butterfly from the plate offered him.

"I don't believe I have ever seen such before. They certainly look good."

One bite made him more than pleased to take another and another, until he was quite as enamored of the cakes as the rest of them. He matched Merry's grin and reached for more cakes. Pure mischief danced in Merry's eyes and soon there was but one cake left. Since all were too polite to claim that one, Will handed over his cup and napkin to Nell and turned to Merry.

"Could I take you for a short ride?" he asked.

"I would enjoy that," she agreed. "Wait just a minute 'til I get my shawl and Anna, my abigail."

Soon they were enjoying the evening breezes while Will told them of his uncle's favorite ship, the *Orient Pearl,* which had returned recently. He urged the horse to a good pace. Near the edge of town, he pulled up at a blacksmith shop. A broad-shouldered man poked his head over the double door to greet them.

"What ho, Will? Did your buggy break a spring?"

"No. I beg your indulgence to let us drive out the Old River Road through your farm. The lady and I have some serious talking to do and we'd prefer not to be interrupted."

"Ha! So that's the way the wind blows, is it? My land is yours to use any time, friend. Just don't scuttle your ship out there, you hear?"

Laughing heartily, Castleton jumped down to open the wide gate. The smith called out over the clang of the hammer. "Leave it open. I'm goin' to supper soon's I finish this."

"Thanks," Will called as he sprang up to his seat and urged the horse into motion.

A soft chill permeated the river area. When Meredeth pulled her shawl about her, Will secured the reins in one hand and tugged her closer.

"It is a bit crowded with three in the buggy, but it will keep you warm," he said with a grin as he set the horse to a faster pace.

When they came to a rocky promontory, Will tethered the horse to a tree, then helped Anna alight. She wandered a short distance away to admire the view. After he helped Merry down, Will did not release her but stood gazing at her for several moments. Tenderly he tilted her elfin chin to the right angle and, with feather-light fingers, brushed a wayward curl back from her brow. Her wide eyes deepened to exotic blue-green. There was a world of wonder in her face. His finger trailed down her cheek. How he longed to bury his face in her hair, now lit to glorious gold in the sunset.

"Merry," his voice was low and urgent. "There are going to be times when I must leave to take care of Uncle Reggie's affairs. It wouldn't be fair to offer for you now. I'm not yet able to provide a home for you, but I want you to know what is in my heart. As soon as I can purchase a home and take care of you, I intend to ask for your hand in marriage. Do you. . .can you feel that way about me?"

She lifted sparkling eyes to meet his. "I have never felt so close to anyone before. It may take time to become sure of my feelings, but I do like you very much."

"Will you promise me one thing, Merry? Will you agree that neither of us will marry another until we learn to know each other better and I can be the kind of husband you deserve?"

She searched deeply into his eyes, shining with entreaty, and felt the gentle grasp of his hands on her arms. What would it be like to have those strong arms holding her close, her head fitted into his shoulder?

"Yes, Will, that I will promise gladly and. . .and I would like to know you better."

With a shout of joy, he swung her around until they were staggering from dizziness. His expression grew soft as he dipped to brush his lips across her cheek and gathered her into his embrace. Somehow they managed to climb into the buggy. It was fortunate that Anna came running for they might have forgotten her in their excitement.

All the way back to Mrs. Clairmont's, starlit silence wrapped them in its magic. Anna went inside while Merry and Will said good night.

Holding Merry's hands in his, Will raised each finger to his lips for a brief salute, then folded her hands around the imprint of his kisses. Merry stepped inside to find Nell watching her, a wide smile on her face.

"That be a right young man, Miss Merry. Just remember to keep him close, but not too close 'til he declares himself as he should."

Merry smiled, content to keep their secret to herself for the present. She climbed the stairs with a little skip in her step and closed the door of her room behind her. She had a lot of thinking to do, and the window seat provided just the space she needed. After awhile she saw great, billowing clouds growing into an autumn storm. She remembered that her family often sat entranced by the changing colors in the night sky. Tonight, though, it was not their faces in her memory, it was Will's.

Lightning crackled and sent fingers of blazing color across the heavens. A boom of thunder startled her from her reverie and she sat bolt upright. Wind whipped the trees into a mad whirl. With an eerie cry, a cat sped across the yard. There, just inside the gate, was a cloaked figure, carrying a rather bulky package. A moment later he left, empty-handed. A gentle knock at her door made Merry's heart race faster than her feet. Mrs. Clairmont stood there, looking for all the world like a drowned rabbit.

"My dear, your young man brought this for you through all this deluge. Can you imagine that?"

After thanking her hostess, Merry retreated once more to the window seat. This was much too big to be a message. Perplexed, she tore the paper eagerly. The wrapping underneath held the most beautiful piece of silk cloth she had ever seen. Her fingers traced the embroidery, radiant in the candlelight. A note lay tucked in the folds.

> *My dear Merry,*
>   *This came on the* Orient Pearl. *I will look forward to seeing you wear it. Word came that my uncle is ill. He wants me to come to Boston, but I don't leave until tomorrow afternoon. I have seen you at Christ Church. Look for me tomorrow.*
>   *Will*

Merry slipped the note beneath her pillow and carefully placed the silk in her trunk before surrendering to sleep. The thunderstorm still filled the night with noise and flashes of light, but her dreams were all of blue skies and sunshine, with Will beside her, of course.

By morning the storm had passed. When Merry entered the church with her aunt, she glanced around quickly but did not see Will. She had almost given him up as they rose to sing the first hymn, but when the chorus rang out, there was a shuffling of feet and Will's rich baritone voice joined her soprano as if they had practiced together. The congregation was seated and Merry's cheeks grew warm as Will's eyes held hers. The Reverend Harrison gave an excellent sermon on faithfulness to the beliefs they held. The last hymn was "O Come, All Ye Faithful," reminding Merry that Christmas was very close.

After greeting the Reverend Harrison, Merry was surprised when her papa joined them. "I arrived late, so I had to sit in the back, but I did want to speak with you and Mina before I leave," he said, smiling at Merry.

"Dr. Elliott! How nice to see you." Mrs. Clairmont hurried to them. "Mina and I were just saying how good it would be to enjoy your company for luncheon today. Can you spare that much of your time? And you are invited, too, Mr. Castleton. I promise you some more butterfly cookies."

Dr. Elliott looked doubtful at first but soon was convinced to accept. Will glanced toward Merry; her little nod and bright smile were all he needed to agree.

"I am honored. I have some time before I sail," he said.

When they arrived home, Nell had everything ready for them and Dr. Elliott said grace.

"That is the same prayer my father says at meals," Will confided as the plates were passed.

Conversation came easily among them, and the women managed, with natural skill, to learn a great deal about Will. Far from embarrassed, he told them of his uncle, the ships of their line, and finally his family back in England. His father raised and trained horses for the nobility's use. His mother had her favorite recipes, just as Mrs. Clairmont did. He had not seen them or his brother and three sisters since he graduated from Oxford.

"Did your father train Ahmed?" Merry asked when the last bite of blueberry pie disappeared.

"He insisted I help train him to make a deeper bond between us. My father was usually so busy I saw little of him, except for church each week. Those two years of training were not only a means of becoming friends with Ahmed, but with my father, as well. They are wonderful memories. My mother writes each week and insists upon an answer, so we are still a close family. How about your folks? Do any of them live nearby?"

"My mother died of a fever when I was twelve. Aunt Mina came to us to assure I had the proper bringing up. There's just Papa, Aunt Mina, Matt, and me."

"Matthew is off fighting with Washington. We don't see much of him," Dr. Elliott swiftly explained, "and I must return to my duties. I pray for good news about your uncle's health when you reach Boston. It was interesting to talk with you, Mr. Castleton."

With Dr. Elliott's departure, Will was reminded of his own journey. "I must go, but thank you all for inviting me today. I enjoyed it immensely."

"Will you be here for Christmas?" Merry asked as they said good-bye.

"I cannot promise that, Merry, but I will certainly be wishing I were here. Take good care of yourself. If you dance at any balls, pretend you're dancing one waltz with me, please."

With Aunt Mina standing by, Will held Merry's hand to his lips for a last kiss, then set off at a fast pace.

❧

The weather changed abruptly after that; winter moved in, cold and wet. Merry and Aunt Mina had no warm clothes with them, so Elvira led them to the attic, filled with chests and boxes. Merry found a blue cloak and hood, warmly lined with soft white fur; there was even a muff to match. A fur cloak trimmed with red braid took Aunt Mina's fancy and the maids were each given sturdy cloaks.

Weeks went by with no word from Will or Jim Hanks. One evening, when Merry returned from the hospital, Nell held out a small packet.

"This gent handed it to me at the back door. Didn't say much, just that it was for you, Miss Merry."

Meredeth simply said, "Thank you," but she thought Nell knew a lot more than she told.

In the privacy of her room, Merry opened the missive. As she read, dread washed over her and her hands shook for the note warned she must be cautious. British authorities were searching for anyone sending information from the city. Some had been questioned already. Merry vowed she would go early tomorrow and deliver the message to Mrs. Wilkins.

During the night it snowed; at least three inches lay on the ground and more fell steadily. Merry got dressed and donned her half-boots in preparation to go see Mrs. Wilkins. While eating a bowl of oatmeal, Merry mentioned telling Jesse of the butterfly cakes and the child's wish to taste one. Nell, who had baked a large batch yesterday, offered to send some of the sweets for Jesse.

With the message tucked into her petticoat pocket, Merry and Anna hurried to the back of City Tavern. Much to their chagrin, that gate was locked and that meant that they must enter the common room, filled with Redcoats!

Staunchly ignoring the British soldiers, Merry and Anna marched through the common room and to the kitchen door. But, as soon as they entered, her bag was torn from her hand and she was pushed against the wall. Anna screamed. Startled, Meredeth raised indignant eyes to confront Major Hastings. His florid face was set in stern lines and a sneer twisted his mouth.

"What a pleasant surprise," he said. "I have missed your pretty face around here for some time, Miss Elliott. What brings you out on such a cold day?"

"Major Hastings, keep your hands to yourself. You have no right—" she sputtered.

"Oh, but I do have the right, my dear. You see, I have been ordered to find traitors amongst us."

"Why should that concern me?"

"Spies often appear most innocent. You have been consorting with some of our men. What better way to pry out information, hmm?"

"I did not instigate those friendships. They approached me. That should prove your case is ridiculous."

Anna found courage to say, "That's right—"

Hastings shoved her aside. "All women are born temptresses. They know how to entice a man."

"Like yourself, sir?" Merry demanded. "I have done everything in my power to discourage you, yet you persist in molesting me."

With a livid snarl, he lunged for her, grabbed a fist full of her hair, and forced her head back against the wall. Screams from Mrs. Wilkins, Jesse, and Anna brought instant reaction from the common room. The door was slammed back and several officers rushed in.

"Major Hastings, sir, what—" The young officer swerved to a stop.

Hastings clutched Meredeth to him and covered her mouth with his. Eyes wide in outrage, Merry beat at his face and shoulders, but her struggles only incited his fury. Mrs. Wilkins grabbed Jesse, who was pounding small fists in Hastings's side.

Eyes wide, Anna cried out, "Please, someone help her!" Hastings looked up, his eyes hard. "Do any of you dare challenge me?" he roared.

More men poured into the room. Most of the younger officers stood undecided, but one man pushed his way through the group and stood before Hastings.

"Yes, I think I must, Major. I happen to know this young lady and she is no spy. Now, unless you want me to bring charges against you, release her immediately. In any case, General Howe must hear of your conduct. You go too far."

Turning to Mrs. Wilkins and Jesse, Major Henry Stanfield gentled his voice, "Will you tell us what has happened here, please?"

"You can't take the word of a servant over mine. I am—" Hastings sputtered.

"I know your name and rank," Stanfield retorted. "Let the women talk."

Bereft of speech for the moment, Mrs. Wilkins stood silent. Suddenly, chin jutting out like a ship in full sail, Jesse pulled away and stood defiantly.

"Please, sir, Miz Elliott didn't do none of the things he says. He jus' grabbed the bag from her an' pushed her into the wall. Then he kissed her but she tried to stop him."

Terrified, Anna nodded her head in agreement.

"Thank you, child, for your honesty and courage. I will make sure there is no retaliation against any of you. Now, Hastings, will you explain why you attacked this lady?"

"She's a spy, I tell you. Why else would a lady come to the kitchen like this? She carried a bag, no doubt a ruse to slip messages to Rebels. I have orders to detain any I suspect of passing information."

"Is this the bag, Major?" Stanfield asked as he bent to pick it up from the floor.

He held it above the table, letting the contents tumble out. A half-dozen sugared cakes fell for all to see.

"My butterflies! She brought my butterflies, Mama. Aren't they pretty?"

An undercurrent of chuckles erupted from the other men. They sobered immediately at a glance from Stanfield.

"Your accusations are false, Hastings. I must insist you release this young lady at once."

Glaring at the men who had laughed, the red-faced major removed his hand from Meredeth's hair. She backed away, her eyes huge and full of sparks. Anna replaced the cakes in the bag and Merry handed it to the child.

Hastings growled, "Get out of my way!" and stomped out

the door, his face twisted in rage.

"I think we can all return to our food now. This display is over, men," Major Stanfield said quietly.

When the room cleared of Redcoats, Stanfield crossed swiftly to Merry, easing her down to a chair. Her eyes were still dilated in shock and tears streamed down her cheeks.

"Do not think all Englishmen are like Hastings. Howe will not put up with conduct like this, even from a distant cousin," he assured them.

Mrs. Wilkins brought a cup of cool water. Jesse knelt beside the chair, patting Merry's arm.

"Miz Merry, please be all right. I 'preciate you bringing me butterflies."

After a wrenching shudder, Merry sat straighter and breathed more evenly. "Thank you, Major Stanfield, for your intervention. Just his touch makes me feel as if snakes crawled over me."

"An apt description. Now, if you are feeling more the thing, may I take you to your father?"

"That is thoughtful of you but my coachman waits for me outside."

"Then allow me to escort you. I would be sure you are protected before I leave."

"Thank you. If I could just speak with Mrs. Wilkins and Jesse a minute."

"I will make sure Hastings has taken his leave," Stanfield promised as he left.

When the door closed behind him, Mrs. Wilkins whispered, "You'd best not bring any more messages. No tellin' what that devil will do. They're watchin' everywhere."

"Oh, Miss Merry, be careful," Anna murmured.

Meredeth looked to the door, then removed the packet from her petticoat. "They told me this is the last one. It is getting too dangerous. Can you handle this without putting yourself or Jesse in jeopardy?"

The cook's troubled face suddenly beamed. Grabbing some

bread dough from the table, she inserted the small note, then folded the dough around it, molding it into a butterfly. She sprinkled some sugar on top and slipped it to the bottom of the bag.

"Ain't nobody goin' to notice that under all the rest. They've already seen what was in that bag. Now, Jesse, you skip out the back door like you're goin' to play. Sit there for a minute and eat one of the cakes. Don't be in a hurry, but soon's you finish, you head right home. No dawdlin', now."

"Yessum," the child replied, winking at Merry. Saucy as a chipmunk, she sat on the porch with the goodies in her lap.

Merry clasped hands with the cook. "Thank you for being a true Patriot and friend. I may not see you for a while, but I will think of you and Jesse often."

Head high, Meredeth tugged Anna behind her and across the common room and stepped outside. Major Stanfield leaned on the carriage, talking to Jeremiah. As the Englishman helped her up, he spoke softly.

"May I call on you this eve?"

"Of course. You are always welcome at Mrs. Clairmont's."

He kissed the tips of her fingers, then stood back to watch them leave. Merry felt secure once again. She had a deep respect for some of the British. Her papa was right, but then he usually was.

seven

Merry did mention to Mrs. Clairmont and Nell that they should take no more messages for her to deliver. Still, she could not erase the fearful memory of Major Hastings. Why did she have this certainty that he watched her wherever she went?

At the hospital the next day, it was a struggle to appear cheerful. When her papa handed her the mail, she gladly left a dreary routine of changing bandages and feeding those who could not help themselves. There was a letter for Red Mac. She smiled as she approached his pallet.

"Well now, lassie, you've come to make my heart happy. I wondered how I could amuse myself the rest of the day."

"Will you read or shall I?" she asked.

"I'd much rather hear your sweet voice, if you please."

Merry began with a smile, but when she reached the last paragraph, her voice faltered.

"I fear 'tis not good news, my friend." When she did not meet his gaze, he leaned closer. "Just tell it out, lass. It's better that way."

Clearing her throat, she continued, "It grieves my heart to tell you this, Son, but I dinna want you to come home not knowing. Mary Duncan was wed to Jamie Fergus this day. She said she would be an old woman afore you came to her. She could'na wait longer."

Red Mac's face whitened and he closed his eyes for a few seconds. When he looked at her, his chin firmed in calm acceptance. He patted Merry's hand with a weary gesture that brought mist to her eyes.

"Och now, don't you be acryin' over a big lump of a Scotsman like me. I've weathered harsher storms than this. I well

75

know there's a chance I may never walk again wi'out sticks to hold me up. That would be a hard thing for a bonny lass to love. 'Tis better this way."

"You would be a fine figure of a man even with crutches, Red McClanahan! If I hadn't already given my heart, I'd be tempted to marry you myself. You're good and kind and you have a gift for making people around you happy. She is the loser in this."

Meredeth's outburst brought a whoop of laughter from the Scotsman.

"If Will was'na me best friend, lass, I'd grab you up and carry you off in a minute. By me granny's pipe, Will is a lucky man. I thank you for your caring."

A chorus of clapping hands startled Merry, and she looked up to see most of the patients grinning at her. Across the room, her own papa stood very still, a quizzical look on his face.

"Oh my," was all she found to say. In truth, she had said far too much already. With flaming cheeks, she fled the room.

A few minutes later, she entered her father's office. He did not appear angry, just surprised.

"That was a stirring bit of oration, my dear. I'm afraid I've been so busy I didn't notice my only daughter has given her heart to some fortunate man. I don't even know who he is. Something as important as that should be shared. Sit and tell me, child."

"Papa, I—"

"Never fear. I'm not angry. I'm ashamed I have been too occupied with a war to know my own family. I will do better."

She sat. After twisting her handkerchief so it was wrinkled as a washboard, she raised her eyes. Her papa's caring look sent her flying into his arms.

"Papa, I love you so much. I didn't mean to keep anything from you. We only promised not to marry another until we had a chance to know each other better."

"It surely isn't Stanfield. You met him only recently."

"He is very nice, but no, it is not him. It is Will Castleton."

"The young man who helped bring my things from Conners Inn? Let's see, he shared Sunday dinner with us one day, didn't he?"

"Yes. His uncle invited him to join his shipping business in Boston. He is there now. His uncle is ill and called him back."

"This is the one who goes to Tory parties?"

"Yes, Papa, but he is not at war against us. He is kind and gallant and. . .and I trust him. Mrs. Clairmont and Aunt Mina both like him."

"Then I am sure I will like him, too. Merry, it was hard for me when your mother died. I have immersed myself in my work, but I don't want to lose the closeness we've always had. I will always take time to talk to you."

"I know that, Papa. You are always close to my heart."

"Well, my dear young lady, I fear I must return to work. You will bring your gentleman around when he is in town so I might get to know him better?"

"Of course, Papa."

With that promise between them, Dr. Elliott resumed his rounds while Merry, Anna, and Dela donned their cloaks. Their carriage awaited them.

 près

The promised snow fell all the next day and the day after that. Iridescent reflections of bright sunlight changed Philadelphia into a living Christmas display. As Merry went about her duties, she began to wonder how she could make or purchase gifts for her family. Would Will come for the holidays? She would have to find some linen to make him a shirt. She was positive that the fabric he had given her would make a lovely gown with some left over for a reticule. Aunt Mina would like that. Perhaps there would be enough to make a similar one for Mrs. Clairmont.

"Food!" Aunt Mina groaned. "There will be no Christmas goose this year. We'll probably be fortunate to have stew."

"Meat is becoming very scarce. Why, last week there was

not even a fish to be had at the market," Elvira sighed.

They must be content with what they had. Merry was well aware of the scarcities this winter. The minister was right about Mrs. Clairmont. Often a knock at her front door would result in a trip to the cellar or the attic to find help for those less fortunate. One day a much greater call for help came via the grapevine. Washington was asking for cloaks and blankets. Some folks said that his men did not even have shoes but had to tie rags around their feet.

Local residents passed the word from one house to another. They had extra cloaks and blankets, but the problem was collecting them and getting them to Washington. He and his men were but fourteen miles away in Whitemarsh, but with none allowed to leave the city, it seemed hopeless.

"Where are Craig and Clark when we need them?" became a familiar query around town. No one had heard of them recently.

When this word came to Meredeth, she spoke to her papa.

"I may be able to get in touch with Craig or Clark through Jim Hanks."

"How do you know Hanks?"

"Do you remember Jesse and Mrs. Wilkins at City Tavern?"

"That was the cook wasn't it?" Papa asked.

"Yes, they are related to him. She might know where they are."

"I can't like your getting mixed up in this, Merry. Do you think she'd tell me?"

Memories of Hastings convinced her to agree. "I'll write a note introducing you to them." At her papa's nod, she quickly penned a letter to her friends.

It was a long time before the doctor returned. His eyes were troubled as he led her into his office.

"Your friends are gone, my dear. No one seems to know what has become of them. Stanfield was there, but he knew nothing. The officers loudly complain of the food there now."

"Hastings," Merry muttered.

"Is he the one who has been questioning folks lately?"

"Mrs. Wilkins said he'd been watching them. He is a beast."

"Do you think he might have arrested your friends?"

"I can only hope they have hidden where he cannot reach them."

"There's to be a meeting tonight. I'll ask some of the men. Perhaps they will know."

When Jeremiah came for them that eve, he wore a long face but only shook his head when she asked if he were ill. Shrugging, she entered the house, hoping to learn what was wrong. The scene she walked into was certainly not what she expected. At least ten women sat in a makeshift circle, teacups in hand.

"Come in, Meredeth, and join us. I believe we have a plan."

In a daze Merry sat. Mrs. Clairmont appeared to be the instigator of the plot. The women listened eagerly.

"Walsh, the printer, the brewer's son, Horace, and Conners, the innkeeper, have all been collecting blankets, shoes, and clothing for sometime. However, it would be extremely difficult for any of the men to get the load to Whitemarsh. Anything going in that direction will be under suspicion."

There was a general bobbing of heads in response.

"Now Mrs. Graham has a daughter and four grandchildren up in Horesham. They have chicken pox and the Brits already signed a pass for her to go help them. I won't mention names, but a farmer has offered his wagon, which has a false bottom in it. In view of the trade in smuggled goods up Boston way, we won't ask how he happens to have that, either."

A round of chuckles made Merry smile and shake her head. Leave it to Elvira to know about that!

"Mrs. Graham has agreed to take the wagon, but she cannot drive. Would any of you ladies offer to go with her?"

"I can drive," one matron spoke up, "if you get me a pass to show the Brits when we're stopped."

"Excellent!" Mrs. Clairmont beamed. "Will they allow two on your pass, Mrs. Graham?"

"General Howe knew my father back in England. I think I can persuade him to do that."

"Then our plan is complete. Nell, will you please pour each of us another cup of tea. We will drink a toast."

Elvira rose, holding up her cup just as she had seen her husband do on occasion. "May Britain go limping home and let us get on with our lives."

"Hear! Hear!" they all replied stoutly.

When the women filed out to return to their homes, Meredeth knelt beside her hostess. "You are an amazing person. I am so proud to know you."

"Mrs. Pringle suggested I might be getting too old for this. I guess I showed her!"

"Indeed, you did," Merry agreed, hugging the thin shoulders.

ಠ

Two evenings later Merry, Anna, and Dela came through the door, shaking the snow from their cloaks. Their laughter swiftly stilled when they noticed that both elderly women had tears in their eyes.

"What happened?" Merry asked.

"Just minutes ago word came that Mrs. Graham is safely with her family in Horesham, but Carrie Grinnel, who drove the wagon on toward Whitemarsh, was stopped by Redcoats. They were spying out the area."

"What did they do to her?" Merry asked breathlessly.

"They found the secret compartment and questioned her for sometime. She told them some of the women wanted to send warm clothes to their menfolks."

"Was she arrested?"

"They finally released her, but she will never be issued another pass and the wagon was smashed to pieces."

Gloomily they sat around the table to eat, but talk was desultory. Merry soon excused herself and went to her room.

One look out the window at gray clouds fading to utter black induced her to pull the curtain across.

"No matter what we do, it seems the British are right there to thwart us. Will we never win our freedom?"

Shivering in the woolen robe that Elvira had loaned her, she sought the warmth of the Starfire quilt. A full moon outside promised frost before morning. Even in sleep she felt chilled, a parade of terrible dreams plaguing her rest.

The next day Merry, Aunt Mina, and the maids walked to church in silence; the sparkle on the snow went unnoticed. Not many of their friends had smiles to share. Merry sang the old, beloved hymns, but nothing broke the ice of sadness in her heart. Papa stopped by after church.

"They say Washington may move his men. Perhaps he has found more secure winter quarters. Whitemarsh is so close to Philadelphia. Howe might take it into his head to make a raid on them."

"Surely there must be a place in the hills where they would have more protection from the cold. Papa, do you truly think we have a chance to win against the might of the British Empire?"

"My dear, there is always a chance when men determine to make a change in their lives. Very small armies have triumphed over great nations. Washington is a skilled leader. I think much of the trouble is getting the men who do the speaking and the men who do the fighting to work together. They have been quibbling for weeks over sending help to the general and his men, but nothing has been done. If a few of the speakers were put in the front lines, it might change some of their ideas."

"I hope they decide soon," Merry murmured. "Sometimes I wonder if it is really worth all the killing and damaging of property and living with the Brits watching every move you make."

Her papa's voice was very soft and gentle. "Would you rather have the English ruling over us again, passing taxes that do not allow local businessmen to make a living, and treating us like so many slaves to provide their wastrel lifestyle?"

With a strong shake of her head, Merry answered, "No, Papa, you're right. I've just been so discouraged lately, I can't think straight."

"Never forget to pray, Merry. God can do so many things that are impossible for us to accomplish. If it is right that we should be free, and I truly believe it is so, God will provide a way."

"Papa, will you pray with me?"

"Gladly, Merry. I do miss our family devotions when Mama was with us," he replied, circling his arm about her.

"Lord God, Creator of all things, we seek Your help. Our world seems intent upon ruling over others. If it is Your Will, help us to be free of the bondage, free to live without violence, a people serving You only. Bring us out of this valley of death and destruction. Show us how You would have us live and worship You in freedom and grace. Give us Your strength, Lord, and have mercy on us. In Christ's name we ask it. Amen.

"Now hold that chin up and let me see you smile," he ordered, his eyes twinkling.

eight

For over two weeks they heard no gunfire, no mention of battles won. Merry, Anna, and Dela took turns helping at the hospital because there were fewer patients. The younger set converged on the library at least once a week, but the foul weather today made that unlikely. Merry sat in the window seat staring at the whirling snow until a wind-whipped cloak at the back gate brought her upright, nose against the pane. It was Jim Hanks!

She hurried down the stairs and into the kitchen, just in time to see Nell hanging a snowy cloak over chairs by the hearth. Jim was already chewing on a dried apple and some bread still warm from the big brick oven. Without a word, Nell pulled up another chair and motioned for Merry to sit.

She was about to burst with questions. When Jim had swallowed the last bite, he was bombarded from both sides.

"Did Washington move yet?"

"How did you know I stayed here with Mrs. Clairmont?" Meredeth blurted out, suddenly realizing she had never given Jim Hanks Elvira's address.

Jim's demeanor was serious, a portent of trouble. He answered neither of their queries and did not meet their eyes as he growled out information. "We knew the Brits kept war prisoners at the Walnut Street prison and on ships. The prison was overflowing with men wounded at Brandywine and Germantown and one prison ship was destroyed when they took Fort Mifflin. We heard they moved the survivors to the top floor of the State House. I went there with a repair crew today." He covered his face with his hands, muffling the rest. "I've seen cleaner sewers. God help those poor miserable men!"

"Did you see anyone we know there?" Merry asked softly.

"Most looked like they hadn't been fed in a month. It was hard to recognize anyone."

"Jim, do you know what happened to Mrs. Wilkins and Jesse?" Merry asked.

"They're not in Philadelphia. We got them out awhile back."

"Could you maybe bring us a bit of meat someday, Jim?" Nell wanted to know.

"I'll try. The farmers don't come in lately. The old High Street Market now serves as stables for British officers. You know marshy old Franklin Square has long been a burying place, but it is filling rapidly. Ben Franklin's *Gazette* and several other papers are doing their best to get a list of the dead Patriots, though few names have been revealed yet. If I'm lucky, maybe I can bring you some meat in a week or two. Can't promise though. It's getting tough to get. Sorry, I gotta go."

He was out the door, jerking on his cloak as he ran, before Nell could hand him a bag of bread. Merry and the cook exchanged worried glances.

"Wouldn't it be grand if he could find us a chicken for Christmas? And maybe some oranges," Nell said, wiping at her eyes with her apron.

"I'd even welcome a crow," Merry groaned as she stumbled upstairs again.

Anna awaited her at the door to her room. "Is there anything I can do for you, Miss Merry? I finished all my chores and I don't feel right just sitting. Could I put your hair up in a new way? Lord Stanfield might call and take you to another ball or something."

"I haven't seen or heard from him, Anna. Well, see what you can do with my hair, just in case."

As if they had conjured up his presence, Major Stanfield came to call that eve. After the usual welcome, plus a plate of butterfly cakes that appeared by Nell's magic, Stanfield gave them some good news.

"I am pleased to report a British ship is due in Baltimore tomorrow. There should be a goodly supply of food in the hold. I shall see that you have some treat for the holidays. I know food has become scarce of late."

"Why, how thoughtful of you, my lord. What a delight that will be for all of us," his hostess responded.

"I cannot stay long for I am shortly to report for duty. Miss Elliott, there is to be another ball this Saturday eve. Dare I hope you will allow me to escort you?"

Merry smiled as she answered, "Yes, my lord, I would be delighted to accompany you. Where is this one to be held?"

"Mr. and Mrs. Carruthers have invited a number of the officers to their home. Are you familiar with that family?"

"The Thomas Carruthers family?" Merry asked. "I went to school with Cecelia, though I have not seen her lately."

"She will announce her marriage to a captain in my command. Forgive me, but I must take my leave. They have kept us busy lately with guard duty."

At his request, Merry accompanied him to the door. He stood, awkward and embarrassed for a moment, before meeting her gaze. He handed her a card.

"Please, don't misunderstand my motives. I cannot help but be aware of the difficulty of finding fabrics here. I know you came with few gowns. If you will visit this dressmaker, she will make a gown for you of whatever material you choose."

Cheeks aflame, Meredeth shook her head. "Thank you for your offer, but I cannot allow you to do this. My other gowns are at home, but it is impossible to get them. I will simply wear what I have."

"Where did you say your estate is?"

"Cresswick Manor is a two-and-a-half- to three-hour ride northwest of Philadelphia."

"Hmmm." He rubbed his chin thoughtfully. "I'm off duty tomorrow. Do you have any plans for the day?"

"No. I am not needed at the hospital lately."

"Very well then. We can make an outing of it. Will you

accept my escort?" Stanfield asked.

Merry's eyes danced at the thought. It had been so long since she had ridden. . .then her face fell. "My horse. . .we came in the carriage."

"I can borrow a mount from one of my men. Captain Severn is promised to a card game tomorrow. His horse is a bit frisky, though."

"I am an avid rider, my lord." Merry grinned reassurance. "I will find a more placid horse for your abigail. My valet can do without his steed for one day."

When Stanfield left, Merry excitedly reported the news to the others. Nell packed a basket lunch for them. It proved to be a perfect winter day, cold but bright with sunshine. The trio set out in great spirits, allowing the mounts their heads. The major had no problem exiting the city's boundaries.

As they neared the manor, Meredeth eagerly watched for some sign of life. Had Mrs. Tulley and Barnabas taken the cattle to Cousin Ferdy's? Was the family silver hidden? Not that she expected Stanfield to appropriate them, but he might mention them to others. At least their home still stood intact. Two figures appeared on the veranda.

The riders heard Mrs. Tulley cry out, "It's Miss Merry, the Lord be praised! And Anna, too, I declare."

The housekeeper ran toward them, arms outflung. Swiftly dismounting, Merry ran to embrace her.

"Oh, Miss Merry, is everything well with you and your family?"

"We are all in good health. Mrs. Tulley, Barnabas, let me introduce our escort, Major Henry Stanfield. We have need of more gowns and he was kind enough to bring me here. Barnabas, can you find Papa's boots and a warm cloak for him?"

"Sure will, mistress, soon's I show the major where to stable the horses."

While Stanfield and the old man strode off, Meredeth hugged the housekeeper and urged her inside, where they could talk quietly.

"Mrs. Tulley, we brought a picnic lunch. Can we eat here on the veranda? We don't have much time. I want to choose some gowns for Aunt Mina and me."

"I'll prepare a table for you, Miss Merry. Anna and Abel, the stableboy, can get trunks from the attic. And don't you worry none, mistress, your silver and the cattle are all at your cousin's place, though nobody has come here 'cept two soldiers. They asked for something to eat, but they didn't bother anything."

"They were probably seeking horses. Thank you for sending our stock away. Do you have enough food here, Mrs. Tulley?"

"I put up lots of green beans, peas, and potatoes from the garden and your cousin sent some chickens back with Barnabas. We'll manage for the winter. Is food scarce in Philadelphia?"

"We are staying with an old friend of Aunt Mina's, but the farmers haven't come to the market much lately."

"Well you just go find the clothes you want to take and I'll put together a bit of food for you. Your cousin checks now and then to see if we need anything," Mrs. Tulley assured Merry.

"Thank you. We will all appreciate that. I'll go pack our clothing."

Merry had never before realized how much her home meant to her. She looked at her mama's portrait for a few minutes, then set about gathering what they would need. Abel and Anna brought down trunks and Merry soon had them filled. At the door of her room she paused for a long look, then hurried downstairs. She must get the books Papa wanted.

The picnic proved to be a delight; Major Stanfield was an adept storyteller and coaxed others to contribute. With a last hug for Mrs. Tulley, Meredeth rolled one of her best gowns carefully into a bundle to fit a saddlebag and then they left.

On the way back to the city, Stanfield stopped at a check-point and ordered a guard to deliver Merry's trunks to Mrs. Clairmont's the next day. When the trio dismounted in Philadelphia, Merry turned shining eyes to Stanfield.

"Thank you, not just for bringing our clothing here, but for a wonderfully pleasant day."

"It was most enjoyable for me, Miss Meredeth. I was able to see a bit more of your country. I understand why you love it. Someday I hope I can give you a tour of my home and introduce you to my sisters. This war cannot last forever."

She shook her head. "I doubt if I wil ever get to England. I am promised to a young man here, but I have quite changed my mind about you British. I do not condone what your king is doing to our country, but some of you are very congenial."

With a gallant bow, he raised both her hands to his lips. "Until tomorrow eve then."

Merry stood staring at his back as he rode off with the other horses in tandem. He was an exceptionally nice man. A small voice inside whispered, *Will, why haven't you written? I miss you so much.*

Later that evening, Aunt Mina came to Merry's room to say good night and thank Merry for arranging to get more gowns for them. "So Cecelia is to marry one of the British. Well, some of them are quite pleasant. Hopefully she has chosen well."

"It will be good to see her again. We have drifted apart the last few years. I wonder if she has changed."

"You will soon see. Perhaps this war is nearing an end. It is at least much better without the sound of gunfire disturbing our sleep each night."

The next day, in spite of heavy snowfall invading the city, their trunks were promptly fetched. Merry was glad to have her lacy, silver-threaded wool shawl again for it was warm in spite of its fragility. Her ice blue gown was rather lightweight and ballrooms were not always well heated. She hoped Stanfield brought a closed carriage to ride to the ball in for large, white flakes were falling and being driven by a strong east wind.

Thankfully, he had. Trust him to prepare for just such a contingency. When they arrived at Thomas Carruthers's home, the stairway to the ballroom was so crowded they had to wait sometime to reach the receiving line.

A familiar voice welcomed her. "Meredeth Elliott!" Cecelia Carruthers said. "I'm so glad you came. It has been an age since I saw you. We must find time for a cozy chat." She lowered her voice to add, "Right after the supper dance, follow me to my room."

Nodding her understanding, Meredeth moved on into the ballroom with Stanfield. It was draped with holly and ivy, tied up with red velvet ribands. A small orchestra was playing a promenade. As before, Stanfield did not release her dance card until he had signed for two waltzes and the supper dance. He handed Meredeth to her first partner, then set off to find his friends.

Merry was familiar with many of the officers now and found conversation much easier. The swirling movement of the waltz made her a bit lightheaded as Stanfield claimed her for the supper dance. He twirled her into the hallway and stopped beside a window alcove. With gentle hands he cupped her face. "You mentioned being promised to a young man here. In England that often happens when the participants are children. Yet when they become adults, they change their minds. Is it the same here?"

Merry could not have moved if her life depended upon it. This man was kind, intelligent, and strong, but she did not love him. He was a good friend, no more.

She breathed a silent prayer. *Oh Lord, help me to explain in a way that doesn't hurt him.* "You are a dear friend, my lord, but I made this promise just a few months ago. I love him very much, though I will always thank God for sending you into my life."

Meredeth inched away from Major Stanfield's embrace,

but he captured her hands and held them loosely between his. "Then we will be good friends, Meredeth. May I continue to see you?"

"I would like to count you friend, my lord."

With a resolute sigh, he offered his arm and led her back to the ballroom where several others joined them for the midnight supper. When the music began once more, Meredeth excused herself and hurried to the room reserved for the women.

Cecelia led her down the hall to a spacious bedroom. "Sit here on the bed. I can't wait to show you my trousseau and the gifts he's given me."

Cecelia brought out one lovely gown after another, a sparkling necklace of garnets with matching earbobs, a gold-embossed jewelry box, and a watercolor of the castle that was to be their home.

"They are truly beautiful! Cecelia, tell me, how did you know he was the right one for you?" Merry inquired.

"Oh, he is pleasant to be with. Father says he is one of the wealthiest men in England and Mother is in alt over it. Just think, I will be the Baroness Delverson!"

"Do you love him?" Merry asked softly.

"Well, we've only known each other for a few months. Mother says love will come. At least I will not be left on the shelf when this war is over. So many of our men are dead. I will have everything a girl dreams of."

"Then I wish you the very best. Perhaps we can continue seeing each other and renew our friendship."

Cecelia tilted her chin up, but her eyes failed to meet Merry's. Nervous hands in her lap made a shambles of her lace kerchief. Troubled, Meredeth reached to touch her, and Cecelia grasped her tightly. A sob caught in Cecelia's throat as she leaned forward, afraid that someone would hear.

nine

"Do not speak of this," Cecelia said. "I must tell someone. Delverson says I must be prepared to leave right after Christmas. He is sure our Rebels will be crushed by then and the British troops will leave only a small contingent here to oversee the colonies. Delverson says they have Washington right where they want him, and once he is captured, the rebellion will fall apart. Merry, I am to return to England with him. I'm so frightened. Delverson is nice, but what shall I do in a strange place, knowing no one?"

"You will know Delverson." Merry feared that was spoken with little sympathy. She tried to give some encouragement, while absently patting the sobbing young woman's shoulder.

Inside, though, her mind churned with memory of recent events. Was Washington in danger? He had escaped capture at Fort Miflin and earlier in Boston. The colonists considered the "wily old fox" invincible. No, she could not accept the possibility of his capture or the Patriots' defeat, though England had far more wealth and men-at-arms. Pulling herself together, she tried to ease her friend's anguish.

"Cecelia, remember the dreams we had at school? You were going to marry a great lord and I planned to marry a doctor or scholar. Your dream is coming true. None of us knows much of our future husband's family, but we accept them and learn to live with them. Delverson sounds like a pleasant young man. Think of this as an adventure into a new world and remember that no matter where you go, God will be there with you."

After a few noisy sniffles and a hiccup, Cecelia raised her eyes to meet Merry's. "You are right. Oh, I'm so glad I talked to you tonight. Delverson is a dear and I think I can learn to love him."

Questions still circled Meredeth's mind. She could not help asking, "How can they be so sure of taking Washington?" in a shaky voice.

Her eyes wide, Cecelia gasped, realizing she had confided more than she should have. Setting her shoulders firmly, she lifted her chin to reply, "Everyone knows he is camped at Whitemarsh. It is a perfect trap. The British can easily surround his troops."

"I heard he was there, but I think he may be more difficult to catch than they believe. He has always had an uncanny intuition. In any event, I wish you joy in your marriage."

Together, they returned to the ballroom, where sets were forming. Both were swiftly whirled away.

Later, at Mrs. Clairmont's door, Stanfield did not linger, the sharp wind flinging snow at them even under the protection of the roof. After he left and when Merry entered the house, she found Aunt Mina propped crookedly in a wicker chair, soft snores coming from her open mouth. Merry smiled fondly as she reached over to waken her aunt. There, in the dim light, two long legs came into view. Merry stepped closer, biting her lip to keep from shouting, for beneath the tousled hair of the second sleeper was the face she so longed to see.

"Will," she whispered in his ear, "when did you get here?"

Abruptly he jerked upright, shaking his head to chase away deep sleep. Bleary eyes met Merry's and they both chuckled, a bit embarrassed at the position in which they found themselves. That woke Aunt Mina, who vaguely told them to be quiet. A bit discomfited herself, she rose, twitched at her skirts, and smoothed her hair.

"I shall retire to my bed, where all good people should be at this time of night," Aunt Mina said, glaring at Will, her finger pointed at his chest. "You may remain five minutes, no more. Merry, I will speak to you in the morning. I am far too tired at present."

Will lurched to his feet, urgently smoothing his clothes.

When Aunt Mina's indignant tread was silenced by a closing door, he and Merry stood staring at each other like two fish in adjoining bowls. Finally realizing their allotted time was swiftly passing, he reached for her. Face aglow, she came to his arms.

"How I have longed to do this these last weeks," he murmured in her ear.

She drew back as far as his arm would allow. "Weeks? It's been a month and five days with no word from you."

"Has it now?" he said softly but with a twinkle in his eyes. "Then you must have missed me as I have you."

"Yes, well, I truly thought you would write since you were gone so long."

She dipped her head, but he did not want their eyes to break contact. His finger under her chin restored visual communication. With deliberate slow motion, he claimed her lips.

"You taste sweeter than Nell's butterfly cakes. There were so many things to do when Uncle Reggie died, yet through all the rush and sadness I kept seeing your face. I couldn't wait any longer to hold you in my arms. Fortunately I had no problem leaving Boston. Washington's new counterintelligence force has more control over that city than the English do, in spite of their reputation."

"I am so pleased to hear that. A friend told me something tonight that left me concerned about Washington's safety."

"I suppose no one can be counted safe these days, but Washington is no fool. His grasp of human nature and success in fielding an army constantly amaze me," Will assured her.

"I did not mean to interrupt. Tell me more of your uncle and the shipping business. I know so little about either."

Merry snuggled a bit closer, enjoying the scent of the pine soap he used and the warmth of his arms. Will's voice grew huskier as he continued, "Uncle Reggie was a hard man in his business dealings, but he had a soft spot in his heart for me. Whenever I showed promise, he let me know he was pleased. Usually he gave orders and expected them to be obeyed. Even when he elevated me to partner, he controlled all decisions."

"You were gone so long, I feared for your safety."

"It was just as long for me. The memory of you kept me sane amid all the business decisions I had to make."

He relaxed back into the chair, pulling her beside him. "In the end, he provided for all the relatives, but the entire business is to be mine if I run his affairs well for two months. I've been working eighteen hours a day to tie up all loose ends. There is one thing more I must do to prove myself. Uncle's favorite ship of the line is due in port."

"Does that mean you must leave again?"

"I am afraid so. Because of the British blockades, Trent is bringing the ship into Baltimore Harbor instead of Boston. I have buyers coming to meet it and another cargo waiting to go out. It is due in three days, so I must leave early this morn. I had no idea how I would get through the guards, but God provided the way. I met Jim Hanks out near Whitemarsh and he brought me in. Your aunt was none too pleased that I asked to wait for you, but I had to see you, Merry."

The small clock on the mantel pointed to half-past-two. "Jim will come for me around three," Will warned.

"When was the last time you ate?" Merry asked.

"I recall a small meat pie about ten yesterday morn."

"If you have a hard ride ahead, you will need food to sustain you. I think Nell will forgive me for invading her kitchen. Come on. There was some hearty stew left from supper. I'll warm it for you. I may be able to find some of her biscuits, too."

Taking his hand, Merry tugged him through the dark hall to the kitchen. Much to their surprise, a candle burned on the table and stew bubbled in the pot over the hearth. Nell appeared with warm biscuits and a bowl of butter. Two places had been set.

"I jest thought ya might be hungry. They don't always feed ya much at them balls. Well, sit down and I'll fetch some milk from the cellar."

"Thank you, Nell. That was thoughtful of you." Will grinned at her.

"Humph! Don't take no thought to figure two young'uns are gonna be hungry this time of mornin'. I had to do some chores, anyhow. Miss Merry, mind you clean up when you're done now."

"I will. Thank you. You are a dear."

"Ain't never been nobody's dear. If I like ya, don't mind atal doing fer ya and that's that."

Off to bed she marched, leaving them alone. The aroma from the hearth lured them to investigate. Suddenly ravenous, they devoured biscuits and stew with little conversation. When they finally pushed aside the bowls, Will reached for her hands. His thumbs made tiny swirls over their fragile bone structure, though his eyes never left her face.

"Merry, I stopped by the hospital on the way here. Your father and I talked for a while. I inquired if he had any objections to me as a son-in-law." Will grinned broadly before continuing, "He looked down his nose very sternly at me and wanted to know who or what was in control of my life."

Merry's face sobered as she stared wide-eyed at Will. Faintly she asked, "What did you say?"

"I'll admit I thought hard about that before I answered. Finally I said the only thing I could, truthfully. I told him God had been in charge of my life since I was a small child, and after Him, I loved you more than anyone or anything."

Merry's mouth trembled into a smile. Her eyes danced as she urged Will to continue. He caught her to him in a tight embrace.

"He slapped me on the back so hard it almost buckled my knees. They were shaky anyway. Then he told me to go find you and see what you thought about it."

"That's my papa!" Merry's smile burst into laughter.

"How much time will you need for the Reverend Harrison to marry us properly in church, love?" Will asked.

Merry tried hard to keep a straight face as she inquired, "Is that a proposal, Mr. Castleton?"

"Your pardon, my lady. I have not been able to think properly since I left you. If you desire a formal proposal, you shall have it. Will you marry me, Meredeth Elliott?"

The seriousness of the situation was only slightly marred by a smudge of stew on his chin, the shadowy crescents under his eyes, and the thick lock of hair that plopped onto his forehead as he descended to one knee. At the sight of that cherished face looking at her with adoration, Merry whispered, "Yes, Will. Oh, yes."

One finger wiped the smudge away, while her other hand swept the errant hair back from his eyes. Cecelia could have all the castles in England. Merry wanted only to follow this man to Boston and become a part of the rest of his life.

He caught her hand and gifted it with a kiss. Eagerly she leaned forward into his embrace. Will caught her tightly enough, but they were both off balance and tumbled to the floor as a faint knock at the back door brought Nell hurrying in.

"Well, I ain't never seen a man propose that way afore," she said. "Looks like you found the right words, Mr. Castleton. Sorry to bust in like this, but someone's at the door."

Before Will could lift Merry to her feet, Jim Hanks stood, arms akimbo, shaking his head at them. "You Brits sure have some strange ways. Looks like it all worked out, though. I'm happy for you, but we've got to ride. Howe's got men out skirting the city. I brought your horse all packed up and ready to go."

"I'll be right with you," Will promised, pulling Meredeth up with him.

He held her close as he whispered in her ear, "I love you so much. I'll be back as soon as I can. Talk to the reverend and take care of yourself."

Jim had been standing looking longingly at the biscuits. With a sweep of her hand, Nell dumped the lot into a bag and handed it to him. He rewarded her with a hug, then whisked out the door. Will flung his cloak around his shoulders, took one last look to memorize the face of his future wife, and dashed outside. There was no sound for a few minutes except the beat of pounding hooves and the utter silence that followed. A tiny shudder of apprehension shivered along Merry's spine. Nell gave her a comforting embrace before wishing her good night. The next day several of Mrs. Clairmont's friends came to visit. Meredeth sat quietly as they shared bits of news. No mention was made of arrests or confrontations on the roads during the night. By evening, she felt certain that Will and Jim had made it through the British guards. Now it was just a matter of waiting, but that could be a worrisome thing.

Word came of another meeting of the Patriots. Merry and Anna stayed at the hospital that eve. To Merry's surprise, Red Mac already knew of Will's visit and the promise made between them.

"Och, lass, my Scottish heart couldn't be happier. I knew the lad had good sense and a large portion of luck. May the good Lord bless you both."

A loud knocking at the entrance sent her hurrying to open the door, but it slammed open before she reached it. Three Redcoats pushed into the room. One of them grabbed Meredeth's arm in an iron grip.

"Where is he? Where is the doctor?"

ten

December 1777

Before Merry could answer, another large man pushed through the doorway. It was Jeremiah, and in his arms was a blanket-wrapped figure!

"Miss Merry! Where's your papa? Mrs. Clairmont's been hurt."

Merry was speechless. In shock she looked from one to the other, then said the first thing that came to her mind. "He. . . he went to get some medicine. I don't know when he will be back. What happened to Mrs. Clairmont, Jeremiah?"

Elvira's face was pale. With a wavery voice she explained, "I fell trying to reach a jar on a shelf too high for me." Then with a barely perceptible wink, she added, "Your papa said we should come here. He'll be here as soon as he finds that medicine."

Merry glared indignantly at the man clutching her arm. "Let me go. I must tend to this patient."

The man frowned, but released her. Although he gave his comrades a signal to stand aside, they watched every move that was made.

Jeremiah gently lowered Elvira to the examining table. As if they knew what they were doing, Merry and Anna made her as comfortable as possible, checking first her heart and pulse.

"My ankle hurts something terrible. Do you think I've broken it?" Elvira asked.

Solemnly Meredeth exposed the swollen ankle, carefully moving her fingers over it.

"How long has Dr. Elliott been gone?" one of the Brits asked.

"I. . .I do not have a watch," Merry answered. "It was a short time ago he left."

"There's word out that the townsmen are having a Rebel meeting tonight. Our men are checking everywhere. He'll wind up in prison if he's caught at that meeting," he warned, jerking Merry's arm toward him.

"You will release my daughter immediately! You have no right to mishandle her," a voice demanded.

"Dr. Elliott!" Anna cried out.

Merry closed her eyes and forced herself to take a deep breath. When the Redcoat dropped her arm, Jeremiah tugged her behind him. Papa stepped closer to confront the soldiers.

"What is it you want?" he asked in a quiet voice.

"We heard you went for medicine but I don't see any. Where were you, Doctor?"

"They told you. I was seeking medication. It is, like most things these days, very hard to come by. I found none. As a doctor helping your own men, it seems to me it would be wise for your people to provide the necessary medicines. I will speak to General Howe about this."

The man's eyes flickered toward his companions. Then, with a grimace, he motioned for them to follow as he strode away, muttering under his breath.

Meredeth ran to her papa. When she opened her mouth, he placed his finger across her lips. Hugging her close, he turned to the others.

"Let me see the patient, please."

When he had inspected the swollen leg, Dr. Elliott declared, "It is not broken, but it will need to be tightly wrapped and you must stay off your feet until the swelling is gone. I'll give you some herbs for the pain. Don't put your weight on it for a few days at least."

When that was done, Mrs. Clairmont was taken home and made comfortable in her favorite chair. She soon fell fast asleep and Jeremiah carried her up to bed. The others were about to retire when there was a soft knock at the back door.

Nell reached it first and pulled it open. There was genuine relief all around when they saw Dr. Elliott. He slipped inside and the candles were snuffed out. They all sat around the kitchen table.

"As I neared the meeting place, I saw it was surrounded by Brits, so I hurried back," the doctor told them, "and none too soon. We men must make other arrangements to meet in the future. Thank you all for your help. That was well done. You will not work at the hospital anymore, Merry. I want you to remain here as much as possible."

"Very well, Papa. If Stanfield asks me to go with him, what shall I tell him?"

"You will tell him you are pleased to accept his invitation. I hardly think they will bother you in his company. Friends, we stand in need of God's help. This is getting beyond our control. Please join hands with me.

"Dear Lord God, we come to You with humble pleas. First we ask Your forgiveness for wrongs we have done. We are earthen vessels in Your hands. Fill us with Your Will and Your ways, that we may be reflections of Your grace and mercy. We ask You to please watch over our families and friends. Keep them safe, Lord. If it is Your Will, bring this terrible war to an end so that we may live in peace again. Until then, grant us strength and patience to be Your people in deed as well as in Your Word. In the name of Jesus, we ask Your help. Amen.

"Now I must return as swiftly as I came. Perhaps they will not be so vigilant since they saw me there tonight."

❧

The next week, several folks came requesting aid. Supplies, though, were nearly gone. What sort of Christmas could they have? Unless Stanfield brought something, they would be fortunate to have stew. One night there was a knock at Mrs. Clairmont's door. Mrs. Clairmont greeted a Quaker woman, then asked Nell's help in the kitchen.

It was sometime before Mrs. Clairmont returned and, to

Merry's surprise, her guest was not with her. Mrs. Clairmont's eyes were downcast and a frown marred her brow. She spent the rest of the evening muttering to herself and jabbing at her needlework haphazardly. Merry and Aunt Mina finally excused themselves and went to their rooms.

Snuggled under the Starfire quilt, Merry blew out the candle and settled herself for sleep. Darkness lay thick and heavy; her thoughts were troubled. Something disturbed her awareness. Had someone called her name?

"Merry," the whisper came a bit more urgently.

At first she looked to the window. The trees made wild, scrabbly noises against the house and a bright moon cast familiar shadows.

"Merry, please."

This time she turned toward the door. Chewing at her underlip, she slid from the warmth of the bed and, bare feet cringing on the cold wooden planks of the floor, she turned the knob. The door swung back and a whirlwind of muslin entered. One small hand closed the door while the other reached toward Merry.

"Do not light a candle, child. It goes against all the rules of hospitality, but I need your help desperately. Do say you will do it."

Merry chided herself mentally for it was only Elvira Clairmont. What had she expected? Hastings? "Come, sit on the bed with me and tell me what you want."

Her guest perched, like a recalcitrant bird, on the edge of the bed. Absently she fingered the quilt's pattern. "I used the small one, you know. You are most welcome to do the same."

"The small one?" Merry questioned.

"Oh, yes. It has hidden pockets just the right size, you see."

"The right size for what?"

Mind awhirl, Merry wondered if the dear woman had hit her head when she fell or had been dreaming and was not fully awakened yet.

"Why the notes, my dear. Like the ones you have been receiving."

Merry froze, mouth open like a doomed flounder.

Mrs. Clairmont continued with a sly smile. "Nell told me all about it. Then she said who brought the packets and I knew right off what they were. I've made a few deliveries myself. It was quite exciting."

Meredeth collapsed in a shaking heap, laughter bubbling over like boiling syrup. Elvira watched for a moment before dissolving into giggles herself.

"Well, if that don't beat all! A fine bunch of conspirators we be," Nell said from the doorway. "If you two don't hush up, the whole world will know afore you git the news to the man himself."

"Did Jim want us to deliver a note?" Merry asked.

"Jim hasn't been here lately. It was Lydia Darragh, the lady who was here tonight. You see, she's got a son in Washington's camp and she hates to see him captured. She lives just across the way from a Tory family where General Howe is quartered. Last night they needed another meeting room, so they took over a floor of the Darragh's home. Can you believe it? They made the Darraghs go to bed and set a guard on their room. Then a large group of them met in the room upstairs."

"What happened?"

"Well, you see, the Darraghs need some work done on their chimneys. There is an open space between the fireplace in their room and the one upstairs where the Redcoats met. Lydia heard everything they said. They plan to raid the camp at Whitemarsh and capture Washington. We can't let that happen."

"What can we do?" Meredeth groaned.

"We must get word to Washington. He'll think of something."

"How can we get out of Philadelphia?"

"Lydia knows a way. She feeds a bunch of Howe's men, so she needs flour. A mill just north of here still has some. Lydia is going to take two flour sacks and go to the mill. They'll let her through for that, you see."

"Is this mill near Whitemarsh?"

Mrs. Clairmont shook her head. "It's about six miles from the mill. While the miller is filling her sacks, Lydia will say she has to visit her young'uns, who are staying with their grandma on her farm. Instead, she'll go to a tavern nearby and get one of Washington's patrols to deliver the message to him."

"Mrs. Darragh will do this by herself?" Merry sputtered.

"Well, she wanted me to go with her, but with my ankle hurting just to walk to the kitchen, I can't do it. Could you go with her, Merry? We'd give you a sack for flour, too."

Meredeth remembered the day Matt's note came and how she had prayed to be able to help the Patriots' cause! This was her chance. If they stopped her, she would have a valid excuse to be on the road. She turned a brave smile to her hostess.

"I will do it. Even if it snows, I have that warm cloak you gave me, plus my spencer and my woolen shawl."

Elvira clasped Merry in a hug. The older woman began to cry. "I always try to help others, but I knew I couldn't walk that far. It made me feel so useless. Thank you, my dear."

"You opened your home to help us and you give aid to so many people. You should never feel useless. God works through you in lots of ways. Let Him use me this time."

Elvira wore a misty-eyed smile as she hobbled to the door. "Meredeth Elliott, you are a lovely, Christian young lady. I am so proud of you and I know the Lord is, too. Lydia plans to leave at first light. I'll ask Nell to wake you. Thank you and may God watch over the two of you."

Merry closed the door and climbed back into her bed. She would need her sleep, but she remembered to thank the Lord.

&

Small, scudding clouds along the horizon were already tinged with a faint wash of gold when Merry and Lydia waited patiently for the guards to examine their passes. The wind blew gently, like an old man puffing on his pipe, and the sun's warmth welcomed them. Their passes returned, they were motioned on their way. In the city, neither said much. Now there were only the birds seeking breakfast and a lone horse watching them from the pasture nearby to overhear.

Mrs. Darragh patted the quilted muff with which she warmed her hands. It was Elvira's Starfire pattern!

"Our passes are here. If anything should happen to me, you must take them and the note and slip away immediately. Go to the first tavern beyond the miller's and give it to the proprietor. Tell him it is for Washington. He will understand."

"Do you think someone patrolling the road would search us?" Merry asked.

"Some men would not put hands on a lady, but there are others who find wicked delight in doing so. We cannot take the chance. If we see Redcoats before they notice us, we shall hide. If they see us, I will delay them while you get away. Do you understand?"

At Meredeth's nod, Lydia continued, "My firstborn boy is in that camp. I will do anything to prevent him or General Washington from being taken by the British. At least one of us must get this message through."

"Of course. I will help in any way I can," Merry assured her.

Smiling, the Quaker mother stepped out at a brisk walk. They did not stop until the sun was well up. A cold drink from a creek beside the road refreshed them. Surprisingly the journey went well that morn. Two British patrols hesitated, but when they saw Lydia's Quaker dress and the empty flour sacks, the captain nodded and rode on. Everyone knew that Quaker "Friends" took no part in war. By the time the women reached the mill at Frankford Creek, both were very tired. The miller agreed to fill their bags as soon as he had enough grain processed.

Mrs. Darragh raised a hand to shade her eyes as she said,

"The Widow Kress keeps the Rising Sun Tavern just a little west of us. We're outside the territory usually patrolled by the British. We can walk toward the tavern. It may be we will meet one of Craig's men there."

"Will you recognize them if you see them?" Merry asked as they hurried along the road.

"I know most of them. Hark!" Lydia stiffened as she squinted to see in the distance.

A sturdy beat of hooves approached. It was a lone rider.

"Wait." Lydia caught Merry's hand. "He is not wearing red. Let us stand here and see who it is."

The rider pulled up with a flourish, raising a hand to his cap. A broad grin crossed his face. "Mrs. Darragh. What are you doing so far from home?"

"Charlie Craig! If you aren't a sight for sore eyes! We have a message for General Washington. Can you get it to him swiftly?"

As Mrs. Darragh told him of Howe's scheme to capture their leader, Craig nodded. "Washington heard rumors similar to this from another source. He's got patrols around the area as a precaution, but this confirms it. We'll need to take stronger steps. I have to meet John Clark in five minutes. It may be sometime before I get back to camp. Just over this hill is Tilson's farmhouse. Give the message to Mrs. Tilson. She'll take it to Sergeant Walsh at the tavern. She might give you ladies a hot meat pie if you smile at her. I just had one and they're delicious. Tell her I sent you."

With a wave, he galloped off. Lydia and Merry climbed the hill and soon knocked at Tilson's door. They remembered to smile. When the good woman heard their tale, she urged them to sit and enjoy a meat pie and hot biscuits while she dressed in warmer clothes. They were more than pleased to comply.

"If Sergeant Walsh is not at the tavern, Colonel Boudinot will be. He comes every day for his lunch. I've got a nephew at Whitemarsh. I wouldn't want to see him in a Brit's prison."

In just a few minutes they were all ready to leave. Mrs.

Tilson waved them off, then set out for Whitemarsh. When Lydia and Merry reached the mill, their flour was waiting for them. The bags' weight slowed their return, but they reached the sentries on the north side of Philadelphia before true dark. Both women breathed easier after the men let them through. Mrs. Darragh gave Merry a warm hug as they parted.

"With so many of our young lads risking their lives for our freedom, it makes my heart feel warm to know a young lady like you is so brave and patriotic, too. Your papa will be proud of you."

"It made me feel that I was at least contributing to our fight for freedom. Thank you for giving me the opportunity," Merry replied.

There were only a few blocks to go and Merry hurried to get inside before the British began night patrols each half-hour. She was breathless when she tugged the door closed behind her. Nell had stew waiting and some warm biscuits. Of course they all had to hear about her adventure and, by the time she dragged her weary feet up the stairs, Meredeth was half-asleep. She wrapped the Starfire quilt around her and went to sit at the window to say her prayers.

"Heavenly Father, thank You for walking with us today and keeping us safe. I'm so glad I was able to do something to help our Patriots. I hope it helped Will, also. Please watch over him, Lord, and bring him back to me soon. And please help Papa with all his duties. In Jesus' name, Amen."

Nell must have brought up hot bricks for the bed for warmth welcomed Meredeth as she crawled between the coverlets. Drowsily she vowed she would sleep at least a full day.

eleven

Merry did sleep well, and it was late afternoon of the second day when she became aware of the wood seller's heavy wagon and a whole troop of men on horseback going by. At last her dawdling mind focused her attention. Stanfield planned to stop by tonight!

The coverlets were thrown back, and Merry quickly washed, then donned her chemise and underskirt. Anna bustled in with an armload of fresh clothing.

"Which gown were you wanting to wear, Miss Merry?"

"The peach with the velvet trim, please. What hour is it, Anna? I can smell Nell's vegetable soup."

"It is four of the clock, miss. Here, let me do your buttons. I think there's some other guests right now, but they'll surely be gone before your gentleman arrives."

To her dismay, Meredeth walked into a parlor filled with Mrs. Clairmont's friends, anxious to hear of Merry's jaunt with the Quaker woman. At least she could tell it to all of them at once, Merry realized as she joined the circle.

She whispered to Nell, "I don't know how long this will take. Keep watch and let me know if Stanfield arrives before they leave."

Nell winked and disappeared into the foyer. Merry looked at the expectant faces. For a moment, her mind went blank.

"Meredeth, why don't you just begin when you and Lydia left here?" Mrs. Clairmont suggested.

Taking a deep breath, Merry told the entire tale.

"Everything went so smoothly," she concluded. "I must admit I was very thankful the Lord brought us safely back. Has anyone heard rumors of Washington's plans?"

"We were discussing that before you came. No one has

any idea what he can do. It's so difficult to move a large group of men without the English noticing," Mrs. Clairmont mused. "Meredeth's idea of thanking the Lord is a very good one. Let's all remember the general and his men in our prayers and give our thanks for watching over our friends on their long walk."

After the women left, the conversation turned again to the problems of finding enough food for growing families. It was too early to expect Stanfield, and the aroma of Nell's soup tugged the Elliotts and Elvira into the kitchen. Elvira said grace, then nodded for Nell to serve them.

After the first bite, Mrs. Clairmont's eyes grew large and round as she beamed at Nell. "Why, wherever did you find meat? None of our friends have been able to purchase any for weeks."

Nell busied herself slicing bread, completely ignoring the question.

Elvira took another bite, chewing tentatively. When that was swallowed, she speared a lump from the broth and held it out to examine it. "Mrs. Schoengert, you will please do me the respect of looking at me and answering my question!"

Nell reluctantly glanced at her employer. With a sniff, she murmured, "Little Jamie Conway found a nest of black snakes in his pa's pasture. He and Sam Williker hit them on the head with sticks 'til they was dead. Then they sold them 'round the neighborhood. Sam says they's real tasty, honest, Mrs. Clairmont. An' I done cleaned 'em extra good afore I cut 'em in the soup."

The fork dropped from Elvira's hand. She sat as if turned to stone, staring in horror at the bite she had almost put in her mouth. "Snake? You have cooked us snakes?"

"Well, ma'am, they jus' don't have nuthin' else at market and a body needs meat. That's a fact."

"You know, my dear," Aunt Mina pleaded, "it truly doesn't taste as horrid as it sounds. Take another bite and see what you think. If she hadn't told me what it was, I'd not have known."

"Humph!" Elvira looked from one to the other. Gingerly picking up her fork, she puckered in distaste, squeezed her eyes shut, and nibbled at the piece. A small frown still crinkled her brow, but she managed to swallow.

Then she reexamined the bowl before her. "Well! It's a crying shame when honest folk are forced to eat reptiles. However, I must admit it tastes better if I close my eyes. I suppose we must eat it, but I can't like it."

Merry and Aunt Mina carefully schooled their faces to indifference and continued the meal. Later, as the women sat stitching on their needlework, Nell brought in a berry bread pudding. Mrs. Clairmont complimented her cook and Nell reclaimed her usual look of pride. By the time Stanfield arrived, the atmosphere was one of satisfaction.

"Why, Major Stanfield! How good of you to call," Mrs. Clairmont welcomed him.

"I regret I can't stay long. I have duty tonight. This Saturday there is to be a musical evening at the Lorings' home. They'll have a theater production and several of the ladies will sing or play for us. Would that interest you, Miss Meredeth?"

"I have always enjoyed plays. Yes, I would like that."

"Then I will come for you at seven. I truly must go now, but I'm pleased you will come." He raised her hand to his lips, then left with a smile.

When Elvira went to her room, Aunt Mina stopped by to chat with Meredeth. At the mention of the snakes, they both laughed heartily. The Elliotts had eaten snake before and found it fairly tasty. When her aunt retired, Merry put on her nightgown and retreated to her place in the window seat. She opened the window just enough to smell the pines at the back of the yard. The cool breeze felt good for a few minutes.

From the direction of Whitemarsh, a lone wood duck's call winged over the silence. Normally she enjoyed the sound, but why did it fill her with apprehension tonight? If only Will would return. She missed him. That must be why she was so gloomy.

The expression on Anna's face answered any questions Merry might have asked. She gave one last twirl of her sea green marquisette, then let the dainty folds drift toward her toes. The maid had fashioned a crown of curls, twisted with a narrow strip of lace, and had left one plump coil to trail down her neck to her shoulder.

Just in time, too, for she could hear Nell welcoming Stanfield. Snatching up her cloak, muff, and reticule, Meredeth started down the stairs.

Stanfield halted in the middle of a sentence, just staring at her. "You are exquisite," he said.

"Thank you, kind sir," Meredeth smiled back at him.

It was a perfect beginning to a wondrous night. They were ushered into the Loring estate to find a ballroom filled to overflowing with young people. At one end of the room hung a huge curtain of maroon velvet. Chairs were placed in a semicircle. Slowly the guests moved toward this area.

A very young man stepped forth from the curtain, his eyes aglow with excitement. He took a deep breath, then loudly said, "The Unsung Oracle of Delphia." Curtains were pulled back to reveal three young maids, bowing low. In the background was a painted scene of Philadelphia. The audience applauded generously as the maids enacted a whirling dance of swaying arms and skirts among bowers filled with blossoms.

Music was provided by a string quartet. No one was sure what the tale was about, but it was all beautifully done. Everyone cheered the three blushing maidens and their stiletto-wielding true loves, assuming that all had ended well for them. There were the usual renditions on harp and harpsichord, plus a trio of songs sung by a shy maid whose voice could not be heard above the chatter of the crowd.

Finally a sweet, clear voice captured the entire group. The room became silent but for the lilt of old folk songs and a slight Scottish accent. The crowd responded with enthusiasm.

Leaning over to Merry, Stanfield murmured, "It seems they

saved the best for last."

"Yes, Caroline MacDuff is a wonderful singer. She and I were schoolmates, but her family moved to Boston a few years ago. I haven't seen her since. I wonder if she's living here again."

The butler directed the guests to step into the next room for refreshments, but two words stopped them just a few feet from the cluster of folks around the vivacious singer.

"Meredeth Elliott!" a voice said.

Merry looked up to see Caroline hurrying toward her and saying, "Oh, I so hoped you'd be here and we could talk! Tell me everything that has happened since I saw you last."

When they had embraced, Merry held out a hand to bring Stanfield closer. "This is Major Henry Stanfield, Caroline. Stanfield, meet Caroline MacDuff. You must come visit me, Caroline. I am staying with a friend on Arch Street. Where are you lodged?"

Merry's friend nodded pleasantly to Major Stanfield before continuing, "My mother and I are visiting an aunt who lives on Spruce and Seventh. She's been very ill and Mother has been attending her."

"Why, that is close to the hospital where my papa stays. We've been so near to each other all this time and didn't know it. How wonderful to see you again," Merry exclaimed.

"We enjoyed your singing very much, Miss MacDuff. Do you have an escort?" Stanfield inquired.

"N–no. I came to perform. Mother knows the Lorings and they requested me to sing. Perhaps I shouldn't––"

"If you have no objection, I believe I can find a partner for a foursome and a small table where we can talk," Stanfield said sotto voce.

"That would be just the thing! Thank you, Stanfield. We'll wait here," Merry agreed.

Caroline looked searchingly at Merry. "Tell me quickly before he returns. Are you seeing a British officer?"

Merry's cheeks pinkened. She met her friend's eyes squarely

and chose her words with care. "We are friends. He has taken me to a few parties in town. Papa likes Major Stanfield and thought I should attend some of the entertainments with him. I do enjoy his company. He is a friend of Ben Franklin's."

Caroline hesitated. With a duck of her head, she glanced around. No one appeared to be watching. "Merry, are you a Tory or a Whig or. . .?"

Merry's instant response "I'm a Patriot" widened Caroline's smile.

"Good. I'm surprised you don't have a steady beau. I don't, either, though there's one man I'd truly like to see again. You mustn't ever mention his name. He works for the Patriots. They call him Jim Hanks, but that's not his real name. His whole family is involved in helping Washington," she confided."

"Jim Hanks? I met him recently," Merry informed her.

Caroline beamed. "We danced several times at a party up in Boston and he visited with my family. I heard he was somewhere near Philadelphia, but I didn't know where."

"I think he is one of Washington's couriers," Merry said.

Caroline sighed. "Maybe I'll see him again. He's so interesting to talk to and he's done so many exciting things."

"With Major Hastings haunting City Tavern, Jim doesn't come in town much," Merry advised.

Caroline's eyes darkened as she asked, "Hastings? Isn't he that cousin of Howe's who caused so much trouble in Boston?"

"I don't know about that, but few people here like him. If it hadn't been for Major Stanfield, Hastings would have arrested me as a spy. He swore I carried secret messages in a bag I brought to the tavern. Stanfield turned the bag upside down, dumping out the cakes I had promised the cook's daughter. You should have heard the men laugh! Hastings was furious."

"You were fortunate, Merry. Hastings was behind the killing of a good many Patriots up in Boston. He has an evil reputation. We feared to be found on the streets while that fiend was around."

"Even his own men don't like him," Merry said. "Will says he is an evil person."

"Will?" Caroline questioned.

Eyes twinkling, Merry whispered, "I do have a steady beau. He's English, but he's lived in Boston with an uncle for several years. He's been a partner with him in a shipping business. He's in Boston right now."

"Doesn't he mind your seeing Stanfield?"

"Oh, I think he does, but he can't offer for me until he can afford a home for us. He knows Papa wants me to have a little social life. Also, I've explained all this to Stanfield. He is lonesome for his family, so we agreed to be friends. He's been a perfect gentleman."

Before more could be said, Stanfield and another officer, Captain Richardson, joined them. They carried plates of tempting food. The women were escorted to a small table and Captain Richardson was introduced. He promptly decided to remain in their company.

☙

During the days before Christmas, Captain Richardson invited the three young people to share his box at the theater. Except for the men who had drawn guard duty, all the English troops attended, most with local women on their arms. While they waited for the play to begin, Merry and Caroline delighted in seeing all the lovely gowns, jewelry, and flirting fans. Most of the men wore their regimentals, making the colorful frocks of the women look like jewels set in red and gold braid.

Stanfield directed Meredeth's attention to a couple entering the first box. "Have you ever met General Howe?" he asked.

Merry shook her head. Leaning closer, Stanfield informed her, "He just arrived with several ladies, there in the front box. I believe the matron on his arm is his hostess. Her husband is right behind—"

He frowned, muttering under his breath. Meredeth followed his gaze, wondering what had caused his consternation.

"Forgive me, Meredeth, I understood Hastings had been sent back to New York, yet he is sitting there in all his finery."

Perhaps the man felt their scrutiny for his eyes swiveled to meet theirs. Merry knew the second he recognized them. His body stiffened and a fierce scowl invaded his face.

Merry's hand reached for Major Stanfield's arm. "He. . .he wouldn't make a scene here, would he?"

Stanfield lifted his chin and glared down his nose at Hastings. In the face of that blazing frown, Hastings lowered his eyes, but Stanfield and Merry noted the feral smile that crossed the man's face before he turned back to the woman at his side.

An arctic wave of fear washed over Meredeth. She said no more of the incident, but in her heart she felt pinioned by Hastings's hatred.

❧

Snow fell heavily Christmas Eve. Merry watched the flakes tumbling past her window as she wondered what Will was doing. Had he disposed of the ship's cargo and sent it off yet? Could he possibly make it through the British guard again?

Stanfield stopped by to present Mrs. Clairmont with a fat goose and a bag filled with fresh fruit. Elvira dashed to the kitchen to give the food to Nell. While she was gone, the major presented Meredeth and Aunt Mina each with prettily wrapped boxes. All aflutter, Aunt Mina opened hers to find a lovely woolen shawl, which she immediately tried on.

Meredeth's package was smaller but more difficult to open. After removing several layers of paper, she held up a carved wooden box.

"It's beautiful!" she exclaimed happily.

"You must open that, as well," Stanfield said with a pleased smile.

"Oh, how lovely," she sighed as she lifted out a fan of lace-like ivory with clusters of birds painted upon sheer Egyptian linen, "but we don't usually give gifts except for family."

"We do not do so at home. I wanted to give these as a thank-you for the warm hospitality." He nodded to Aunt Mina. "And for your kindness in accompanying me to parties and such, Meredeth. You have taken away much of the loneliness that plagues a man away from his family. Enjoy your goose tomorrow. I will see you again soon."

Snow was still falling on Christmas Day. Dr. Elliott joined the women when they attended church in spite of the weather. At lunch, Nell proudly carried the roasted goose in to the table. When the doctor said grace, he added a thanks to God for friends like Stanfield.

Merry had stitched lace collars for Aunt Mina, Mrs. Clairmont, and Nell. The cook's eyes nearly popped from her head and she was still admiring hers when she excused herself to go to her room that night. Merry had bought a book for her father. Dr. Elliott produced a pair of ebony combs for Aunt Mina and, remarkably, a pair of blue combs for Elvira. Both women were in alt over the choice. For Merry, he had found a beaded reticule. The Christmas spirit was obvious as they all enjoyed singing well-known carols and remembering Christmases past.

Later, as Merry watched the snow drift past her window, she thanked the Lord for her family and asked Him to send angels to watch over Will. It had been such a pleasant night with her family, but how she missed Will's presence. If he were waltzing, would he pretend that she was in his arms?

❧

Shortly after the new year began, they heard that Washington had succesfully moved his troops to Valley Forge, where, although they had log huts, many doubted that they could survive the winter. More and more snow fell, making movement difficult even in town. Caroline and Merry managed to visit once or twice a week, and the old friendship became much stronger. Merry thanked God for that gift. It helped her forget the ache in her heart. There was no word from Will or Jim

Hanks. Stranger yet, there had been no notice of Matt's death. Because of his spying activities, was he in some unknown grave? Would they ever know his fate?

An unexpected thaw at the end of January brought with it the first serious bout of illness. Most of the city folk sneezed, coughed, or became fevered, and the hospital overflowed with patients. Merry, Anna, and Dela were again recruited to help the weary doctor. Caroline offered her services and was gratefully put to work whenever she could come.

Overwork and lack of sleep finally took its toll on Dr. Elliott. Merry was assisting him with his rounds when her papa staggered, then slid down the wall to the floor. When she touched his forehead, she found it burning with fever. Swiftly she, Anna, and Dela dragged the limp form to a clean pallet and sent for an elderly woman who also assisted at times.

Merry stayed by his side, bathing his face with cool water and giving him herbal tea. What would they do without him? She knew that none of the helpers were able to take over such a responsibility.

A short time later, a matron bustled in with another woman in tow. She approached Meredeth.

"I am Mathilda Atherton. This here's Mrs. Wilcox. We ain't either of us doctors, but I helped my pa with his practice all my life and my friend and I are right handy with herbs and such. If you can use us, we'd be proud to help. We heard you were short-handed."

"Oh, how kind of you! Do make yourselves at home. I've been helping, but I do not know what to do without my papa's guidance. I am Meredeth Elliott. Anna, Dela, and I will be thankful for your experience. Tell us what must be done and we will help you do it."

"Could you show me where Dr. Elliott's casebook is? Soon's I study that a bit, we can get busy here."

Merry showed the women to her father's office, pointed out the ledger on his desk, and let Miss Atherton take over. Papa became Merry's main concern. She sat beside him, wiping his face and chest with cool cloths, but, so far, his temperature remained high. Weary to the bone, she closed her eyes for a minute. Suddenly she awakened with a start.

"Young lady, you won't do your pa any good atal if you don't get some sleep. Now you just march back to his office and lie down," Miss Atherton scolded. "I'll sure call you if there's any change."

With a rueful smile Merry did as she was told. Soon, she was fast asleep.

twelve

February 1778

It seemed as though Merry had hardly slept when a hand shook her awake again. She squinted to see who knelt by her pallet. "Caroline!" Merry said. "What are you doing here in the middle of the night?"

A closer look at Caroline's strained face brought Meredeth straight up, her hand reaching out to the trembling young woman. "What's wrong?" Merry asked.

"Jim's been badly hurt. I brought him in my aunt's carriage, but I can't carry him in. Could your papa take a look at him? He's bleeding so much."

"Papa is unconscious with a fever. There is a lady here helping. I believe she is a staunch Patriot. I will ask her to see to him. Stop crying now. We'll all help."

Quietly Merry tugged Miss Atherton into her father's office and explained the problem. With a sober nod, Miss Atherton swiftly collected her bag of supplies. Within minutes they huddled around the long, still form slumped in the carriage.

"He has a knife slash in his side that is fairly deep. We must staunch the flow of blood, but his pulse is strong and his heart sounds good. It's the fever we'll have to fight mostly. He's too warm."

Merry stood watch while Miss Atherton cleaned out the wound and bandaged it to stop the bleeding. They had almost finished when they heard the rough voices and marching feet of a patrol.

"You two spread your skirts right here over him, one on each side. Quickly now!" Miss Atherton whispered. "I'll roll my cloak and set it by his head and shoulders like this."

She upended Caroline's large bonnet over Jim's head and adjusted her to a sprawled position. "Now, Miss Caroline, you act like you fainted. Miss Merry, you lean over her like this."

By the time the guard reached the coach, Meredeth and Miss Atherton were crowded around Caroline, waving smelling salts under her nose and patting her cheeks as if they were trying to revive her.

"What is the trouble here?" the man demanded.

"Young man, haven't you ever seen a lady swoon? It happens all the time." Miss Atherton leaned over to whisper in the soldier's ear. "They have such delicate sensibilities, you know. She'll come around shortly."

The man lifted a small lantern to look at the white, strained face. With a gruff "Humphh," he returned to his unit. After a brief conference, they went on their way.

"You couldn't have been more convincing if you had truly fainted," Meredeth chuckled, helping her friend up.

Caroline shook her head as she muttered, "I never felt more like expiring in my life."

It was unlikely that another patrol would accost them there. Still, Miss Atherton hurriedly collected her equipment. "Best I be back about my business," she said. "If any comes by with questions, I'll say you went home to rest, Miss Merry. You go with your friend. Get her young man to a safe place and tend him 'til he recovers. We'll take care of things here."

With that assurance, Merry braced Jim's slack figure in the seat. Caroline, the reins limp in her lap, turned frightened eyes to Merry. "I can't take him to my aunt's. He won't be safe there. Where can we take him?"

"Mrs. Clairmont and Nell! He can stay in the spare room. I think they'd let him, if we can get him there. I'll help care for him," Merry offered.

"Oh, thank the Lord!" Caroline sighed.

She snapped to attention and within minutes they were off

at a good pace. They passed a patrol, but the men were busy questioning some pedestrians. The leader gave the carriage only a passing glance.

As they opened the door, Nell peeked out from the kitchen and hurried to help. When she saw who had been hurt, her lips tightened as she muttered about "those Brits." Between the three of them, they dragged Jim's limp body up the steps to a vacant room.

"How did he get hurt, Caroline," Merry asked when they were alone.

"I have no idea," Caroline replied. "I saw him this afternoon in the library. We talked for a long time and he said he had to return to duty. On my way home, I stopped to get some medicine for my aunt. As I came out of her doctor's office, I heard something heavy fall back in the trees on the adjoining lot. No one answered my call, so I walked closer. He was in a heap on the ground. I ran to my aunt's, told Mother I had to help someone who was hurt, and asked for the carriage. She gave me permission, but it took so long to get him into it and I was terrified someone would see us. Thankfully most folks were inside eating supper."

"You go home now or your family will wonder where you are. We'll take care of him. He'll probably sleep all night," Merry assured her friend. Nell offered to peek in on him through the night, so Merry wearily sought her bed. Worries plagued her, but before she reached the end of the list, sleep erased the problems.

She had just filled her bowl with oatmeal the next morn, when Caroline slipped in, quickly closing out the cold wind.

"How is Jim?" she asked immediately.

"Nell has been watching him through the night. Why don't you have some breakfast with me and then we'll both go up and relieve her?"

"You two go on and eat," Nell said as she bustled in. "I came down to fix some broth for that lanky hunk of man. Soon's you finish, go up and tell him how sick he looks. Then mebbe I can keep him in that bed today. He's too frisky for his own good."

"Did the bleeding stop?" Caroline had to know.

"A mite dried on the bandages is all. He'll do if he stays put for a day or two."

When the two women arrived with the broth, Jim was tossing and muttering under his breath, but one sniff of food and he became docile as a lamb. After dunking biscuits into the broth, he popped them into his mouth with the concentration of a dog on a meaty bone. His face reddened at Caroline's giggles but that did not slow him. After the last biscuit disappeared, he laid back against the pillow, a satisfied smile on his face.

"Now that's the way to begin a day. When do I get breakfast?" he asked.

Nell stuck her head in long enough to reply, "You'll get more soon's you prove you can keep that down. Jackanape comes in here and 'spects to be treated like a king!"

Mrs. Clairmont was disturbed when she heard the news. "We can't keep him in a room. I heard they've been searching homes of suspected spies. We'd better put him in the hidey-hole, if he isn't too big to fit."

"Yessum. I already got it cleaned out," Nell agreed.

Jim was able to walk although he made a point of leaning on Caroline's shoulder. By midday they had him safely hidden in the secret alcove. Nell promised to stay with him, so Merry went to the hospital to see how her papa fared. A welcome sight awaited her. He was sitting against a wall, still pale, but his fever had broken.

"You have found me an admirable staff of helpers, my dear." He lowered his voice to continue, "I hear you had an unexpected patient last night. How is he doing?"

Merry laughed. "He is sitting up eating everything in sight and making jokes. The bleeding has stopped. There's no sign of fever as yet."

"He's a strong young man. We'll hope there is no complication. Is Mrs. Clairmont—"

The front door slammed open with a crash and every head jerked to see a troop of Redcoats stomp in. Faces sharp and intent, they scanned the room.

Dr. Elliott pushed himself up a bit. "Is it necessary to create such a clatter? These men require rest and quiet. How may I help you?"

One of them stepped forward. His voice was hard and angry. "We seek one, Douglas McClanahan, a patient here. Where is he?"

"He is in the next room. Merry, will you direct these men?"

Warily she skirted the band, then led the way. "Mr. McClanahan, you have visitors."

The Scot turned with a smile for her. In seconds it was replaced with a sober look.

"That's him. Just pick up the pallet and get him out of here. They'll question him at headquarters."

Merry was pushed aside roughly. In a flash, the soldiers gathered the corners of the pallet, hefted it up along with the wide-eyed McClanahan, and marched from the room. As they passed by Meredeth, one of them thrust a chin in her direction and muttered, "Yeah. That's her."

When the outer door banged shut, Merry ran to her papa. "What is it? Why would they want to question Red Mac?"

A thoughtful frown puckered his brow as he answered, "I don't know, my dear. Have you had anything to do with him outside of the hospital?"

"Not really. He knows Will and he told me if I ever had a message for Will, he'd see that it was delivered. I never sent one. Will! Could he be in some kind of trouble with the Brits? He went to Baltimore to meet one of his ships."

"I'm afraid we won't have the answer to that until Will returns. Merry, don't come to the hospital anymore. You may be in danger. Until I discover some reason for their attention to you, please do not leave Mrs. Clairmont's home."

When the problem reached Jim's ears, he called Merry to him and questioned her for sometime. Caroline soon joined them. It was her mention of Hastings that made Jim sit up with a worried frown.

"Hastings is arrogant, evil-minded, devious, and half-mad, besides! I don't want either of you ladies near him. So Will and Stanfield have both had confrontations with the man and now someone is after you, Merry. It's Hastings. I'd bet on it. Stanfield is English, but he's a good man. I'm glad he's trying to bring Hastings to justice."

Jim suddenly fastened an intent gaze on Merry. "I'll do all I can, but whatever happens, you keep away from Hastings! And that includes you, as well." Jim's hand caught Caroline's and demanded her attention.

They all agreed to keep out of sight and work together. Merry managed a smile for them, then went to her own room. She sat staring out the window. Jim and Caroline were so happy to be together, though he was injured and might be executed if caught. The memory that Will could be involved in something just as serious hit her like a thrown stone. How she wished she could see him, just to know he was alive and well.

&

Several weeks passed uneventfully. The hidey-hole was open and ready and it would take only a few seconds for Jim to disappear into it. He roamed the house, but spent most of his time in the kitchen. Nell was hard pressed to find enough food.

When the women teased him, he retorted, "If you were with Washington and his men, you'd understand what hunger truly is. Did you hear he's moved? What an escapade that was! Washington heard, from several sources, of Howe's attack plan at Whitemarsh. We dug trenches and had our guns ready. Howe slipped out of town late on the night of December fourth, even sent some wagons in another direction to fool any spies who watched. McLane and Washington had a good laugh over that. Howe came marching in on the road Washington said they'd use."

"That was right after Lydia and I delivered the news she'd heard," Merry said.

"Right. The Brit's surprise failed dismally. When they arrived, our men were in ditches with all the guns trained on the Redcoats. The two armies stood there looking at each other for a full day. Howe sent men to reconnoiter, but found no openings."

"Howe is Hastings's relative, isn't he?" Caroline asked.

"He was also the one who led that disastrous charge on Bunker Hill. He knew the deadly aim of the Patriots. Actually we were outnumbered, but we were in more protected positions.

"Next day, about noon, Howe marched his troops back to Philadelphia, 'like a parcel of dumb fools,' one man said. Then it snowed so much, Howe wintered in for the year. That's when Washington moved. Most of his men are used to snow."

"It's so good to hear that kind of story for a change. Have you heard anything about Will?" Merry wondered.

"Don't you worry about Will. He's a canny fellow. Truly he's not part of our army. He just helps at times. The shipping business keeps him busy," Jim told them.

"How does he help you?" was Meredeth's prompt question.

"Oh. . .ah. . .I really shouldn't have mentioned that. Please don't repeat it or I'll be in big trouble."

Merry said no more, but that information made her feel better. At least Will was helping the Patriots, not England.

"Meredeth! Come down, please. You have a visitor."

"I'll be right there, Aunt Mina."

She hurried down to find Major Stanfield, very much ill at ease, in the foyer. His troubled eyes met hers.

"Do come in and be seated, Stanfield. Perhaps Nell can find—"

"Merry, I must talk to you."

Aunt Mina disappeared like a rabbit into its hole. The major took several deep breaths before blurting out the reason for his call, distress flaring in his eyes.

"Meredeth, I don't know quite how to say this. Hastings has been spreading lies about you, claiming you, your aunt, and Mrs. Clairmont are spies for the Rebels. He accuses you of harboring Rebel soldiers in this house."

"Hastings!"

"Yes. The man's gone completely mad. He will do anything to prove those charges."

Stanfield dropped the hat he had been turning round and round in his hands. He leaned toward Merry as he said, "I must know if his charges are based on even the slightest bit of truth before I can help you."

Merry willed her hands to relax in her lap. Like shooting stars, thoughts flashed through her mind. Truly she had spied on no one and Jim was not a soldier.

"How can he think such things when his soldiers patrol so closely we hardly dare step out of our homes, much less the city?"

"Have you ever left Philadelphia?" he asked softly.

"Only that time with you and once with a friend of Mrs. Clairmont's."

"Why—" he began, but she answered before he might ask a question she could not respond to truthfully.

"We needed flour. Mrs. Darragh knew of a mill where some was available. She got a pass and we walked there and back in the same day. The road guards saw us return with the flour. You could check with them."

"Please tell me you did not go to Whitemarsh," he pleaded.

She took a deep breath, long enough to say a swift thank-you to God, before meeting his worried gaze squarely.

"We did not go to Whitemarsh. We went to Frankford Mill to get flour. We had lunch at a farmhouse nearby and then returned home."

Stanfield sagged back in relief. "Very good. Merry, I have seen Hastings gun down people with no more than a laugh of scorn. I have always considered myself loyal to England, but if Hastings ever harms you, I think I will kill the beast.

Promise me you will stay inside this house until he is sent back to Boston. I will do all I can to hasten that day. I must go. We have duty in half an hour. Be very careful, Merry."

She waved him off, her thoughts twisted and knotted inside.

"Is he gone?" Aunt Mina called softly from the kitchen.

"Yes. Did you want to speak to him?"

"Oh no, my dear. We are thankful he is gone."

At Meredeth's look of confusion, Aunt Mina continued, "I mean. . .Oh, Merry, we feared he came to search the house. We practically folded Jim in half to get him into the hidey-hole quickly. I'm sure he'll be pleased to return to his room again. Is something troubling you, Meredeth?"

"I'll tell you all about it later. Let's get Jim out of the hole."

They were all seated around the kitchen table when Merry shared Stanfield's information with the rest. Sober faces stared at each other. Caroline's voice shook. "What if that terrible man comes here with a warrant?"

"There will be no problem," Jim replied. "I am well enough to leave. It is time I reported back to headquarters."

"But, Jim. . ." Caroline objected.

"There is a little matter of unfinished business I'm determined to see completed. I'll return before I leave Philadelphia. Chin up, my girl."

With a sigh, she followed him from the room and by midnight he had said his farewells.

A few tears traced a path down Caroline's cheeks as she turned to her friends with a crooked smile and said, "Thank you all. It is so good to have friends you can depend upon. I'd better get back to Mother and Aunt Bertha. They have been a bit petulant at my absence."

&

It was almost a week before Stanfield returned. Hastings was at least under surveillance. Regretfully, Stanfield informed Merry that his troop had been ordered to outside patrol duty for the next few weeks. Merry's heart sank at the thought of more fighting if the spring thaws came early. He did mention one more item of interest.

"Howe may be leaving us. There is talk that he is to be replaced by General Clinton. I can only hope Howe takes Hastings with him."

In the following weeks, the city's residents heard the boom of big cannon toward the northeast. Could there be more trouble at Trenton or Morristown? There was no word from Jim or Stanfield. Merry thought surely she had worn down at least an inch of her room's floor with her pacing. The view from her window changed to faint green as snow melted and tiny signs of spring appeared. How she wished she could go for a long walk! When her papa stopped by to see them one eve, she fairly leaped into his arms.

"Oh, Papa, it is so good to see you! Are you better now? Is Miss Atherton still helping at the hospital?"

"Miss Atherton and her friend could practically run the place by themselves," he said. "They are gems, both of them. How is my favorite girl?"

"Your only girl had better be your favorite, sir. I am perfectly healthy, but driven to distraction cooped up inside all the time. Could I not take a walk with you at least?"

"I'm afraid not today, my dear. I must return promptly. I came back to get an address of a friend in New York. There is a new sort of sickness taking its toll of the men. My colleague may have knowledge of it. Please bring me my small leather book while I speak to Aunt Mina."

"Of course, Papa," she said, hurrying up the stairs. It took only a few minutes to locate the volume.

An uneasy silence greeted her when she pushed open the kitchen door. A bit embarrassed, she glanced from one blank face to another.

"Is something wrong?"

"Why of course not, Merry," Dr. Elliott smiled. "We were just talking and didn't hear you approach. Thank you for finding my book."

There was something almost tangible in the air. Aunt Mina's hands were fluttery, as if she could not think where to put them. Elvira cleared her throat nervously and sat down, almost missing her chair. Nell spun on her heels and became very busy at the stove.

Dr. Elliott shook his head, smiling at the lot of them. "I suppose it's no use trying to keep it from you. We've all been concerned over Hastings's threats. I've spoken to several friends and they agree we must get you out of Philadelphia as soon as possible. Jim Hanks will help, but he has to work out arrangements first."

"But where would I go?" Merry asked in a startled voice.

"I don't have the answers yet. You keep out of sight as much as possible. Perhaps it is best you do not go with Stanfield. He is doing his utmost to bring Hastings to trial. It might be held against both of you if the top men see you together. I'm sorry, my dear."

As he said his farewells at the door, he tilted her face to look into her eyes. "Perhaps your young man from Boston will be back by then. He might be of help. It is rumored Howe is in disgrace and will be replaced by a man named Clinton. That might solve our problem. Washington's new spy system has evidently been a great success. Between all those good men and the Old Fox's keen mind, I believe we can defeat the British."

thirteen

By the middle of March all Philadelphia turned green in the sunshine and the loons could be heard calling from the marshes again. Nell tapped on Merry's door to tell her that Caroline had come to visit. For a few minutes they chatted of nothing and everything with Aunt Mina and Elvira, then Caroline signaled the need to meet in private. Laughing together, the two women were soon ensconced on the Starfire quilt.

With a serious face, Caroline spoke softly. "I can't stay long but I had to tell you. There's rumors that Howe may leave Philadelphia and some think he will take some of the troops with him."

"But where are they to go? I heard Clinton was to replace Howe."

"Jim thinks Howe will be sent to New York, or possibly Boston."

"But why?" Merry could not help asking.

"There's rumors France might attack England while so many British soldiers are over here. They've been enemies ever so long, you know. The main flank of the Brit's army is based in Boston, but there's a large contingent in New York. If they sent back only half of the men at either place, it would be sufficient to defend England fairly well. Of course, Jim doesn't think highly of Clinton, either."

"Maybe Ben Franklin had something to do with it. He said he would get help from the French."

"I don't know, but Jim is excited about it all. Oh yes, he said to tell you he is sending something special he wants you to take care of for him."

"Something special?"

"I have no idea what he means."

"That's strange. The last message said there would be no more letters because it would put me in danger. Caroline, I'm not supposed to leave the house. Besides, Mrs. Wilkins is no longer at City Tavern. How will I get a message to anyone?" A frown crumpled her brow as another thought came. "Jim is with Washington now, isn't he?"

At Caroline's nod, Merry continued, "Why would he need to send a note to me to deliver to Washington?"

Caroline's mouth opened but no sound came out. She shook her head and whispered, "I don't know. It makes no sense to me, either. I've got to go back, but I'll keep you posted."

Merry sat in the window seat, brushing her hair, her mind a maze with no exit. She shuddered at the stark stillness of the city. As she climbed into bed, the rhythm of hoofbeats kept her from blowing out the candle. It was a single horse, trotting. The hooves slowed to a walk, almost inaudible, coming through the alley behind the house. She heard the rasp of the back gate opening and then a thud.

Without another thought, she slipped out the doorway and raced downstairs. She was just in time to see Nell opening the back door.

"Now whatever made that racket?" the cook mumbled. Leaving the door ajar, she went to her room, no doubt to get her cloak.

Some inner force prompted Merry to grab Elvira's cloak from its hook and tug the hood over her hair. She stepped outside, straining to see in the dim light from the lantern. A trembling spread from her head to her toes. The air was chilly. Goose bumps climbed her spine and froze her heart.

Had Jim made that delivery for her? But then why hadn't he come in? She could see no movement. Was it Jim? Could it be some devious trick of Hastings's. . .a lure to get her outside?

"Dear Lord," she prayed, "send Your angels to watch over me. Help me to know what You would have me do."

A black cloak lurched from the gate. Both fists tight against her mouth, Meredeth swallowed the cry lurking deep in her throat. Tenuous, furtive movements sent her back into the arms of the shadows. But it was no use, for the dark shape came toward her in jerky strides. She should run for the kitchen door, but her feet were imprisoned in the grass. Her heart leaped, almost strangling her with its frantic beat.

It looked as if the cloak reached out. Her own whimper acted as a catalyst of release for her. Stumbling, grabbing at the shrubbery, she pivoted and dashed for the kitchen door, but a dull thump from behind stayed her hand on the knob. Her swift glance revealed a humped cloak on the grass. One white hand lay outstretched as if in supplication. Curiosity overcame her fear and, clutching the post, she eased down the steps.

"Miss Merry, what is it? I went to get my cloak," Nell said.

The warm hand on Merry's shoulder stilled the tremors racing through her body. "I. . .I don't know, Nell. Look! Someone fell out there. What shall we do?"

"Wal now, I'd say the canny thing to do is take a peek and see who it is. Don't seem to be moving. Mebbe someone's hurt. Ain't heard of no ghosts 'round here lately."

Kneeling on either side of the cloak, the two women lifted the hood cautiously. Light from the kitchen revealed a small portion of a white face, nose down, in the grass. Long, dark hair partially slipped from a narrow black band at his neck. Merry lifted a lock of hair from his eyes.

A faint cry escaped her as she sat back on her heels and stammered, "M-Matt! It's impossible but he looks like my brother, Matt. How can this be?"

"Wal from the looks of him, we'd better get him inside or he will be dead. Don't see no blood, but he sure looks pasty. Here, you take that end and I'll take this'n."

When they had him safely in the kitchen and the door locked, Nell set about removing the shabby cloak. Merry's eyes grew large as she brushed her fingers over his face. She bit her lip at the haggard look of him, so pale and worn.

"Oh, just look how thin he is!" Merry said.

"Looks near starved, he does," Nell muttered. "His breathin' is a mite ragged, but his pulse is beatin'."

"Nell," Merry's voice was but a wisp of sound, "I think we'd better put him in the hidey-hole before we do anything else."

The cook nodded her agreement and took the emaciated shoulders from Merry's arms. "You take his legs, real careful now."

They maneuvered him down the narrow stairs and placed him on the cellar floor. Straining together, they moved the big rack of shelves away from the wall. The straw pallet Jim had used still lay there. Gently they lowered the young man. Merry loosened his cloak and opened his shirt, while Nell went up for the lantern and some soft cloths.

The light from the lantern only magnified the extent of his injuries. A deep knife slash had been sewn together with little skill; there were bruises beyond counting; a gash on his head still seeped blood, which had been transferred to his hands and chest.

"It's a wonder he still breathes," Meredeth whispered, wiping tears from her eyes with one hand. "I must go get Papa!"

She leaped to her feet but Nell caught her before she reached the steps. With a gentle shake, she admonished the distraught young woman. "You just think this out afore you run off, child. What if a patrol, or worse, that ornery Hastings should find you out on the streets at night? Let's take a good look, wash him down, and see what he needs first. Then I'll send Jeremiah to get your papa."

"You're right, but we must hurry," Merry admitted, kneeling to help ease off his cloak.

Her eyes blazing with fury, Nell held up Matt's wrists. "Lord, help us. Look at that."

"He's been in prison, hasn't he, chained up like an animal? I wonder how long?"

"I'd say it was way too long, Miss Merry. When did you last hear from him?"

"Just before we came to Philadelphia. That was months ago. How could he have escaped, weak as he is?"

"You didn't see no rider?"

"I heard a horse just before the thud. It sounded different though, almost muted. There was another horse several blocks away, too. It was galloping."

"Mebbe like one was trying to be quiet so's the other wouldn't hear him?"

Merry's eyes met Nell's in sudden understanding. "Someone helped him escape but he was followed! That's why he didn't come in. Do you think Jim. . .?"

"I'd just about bet on it, child. You were right to bring your brother down here first thing. I'm goin' up and turn off the other lantern. We can make do with a candle in the kitchen. There's no windows down here, so no one will see. I'll bring some soap and towels and warm up a bit of broth."

"Thank you, Nell. I truly appreciate your help."

"Nuthin' to thank a body for. Does my old heart good to put one over on them Brits, it does."

Carefully Merry turned the limp form on its side, trying to remove the torn shirt. He groaned but showed no sign of regaining consciousness. His body jerked when she pulled the fabric from his back. He muttered something she could not understand.

At that moment, all the hatred she had felt for the English returned in full measure. She feared to touch the red stripes, but they had to be cleaned. Thankfully the cloths were soft.

"Is it not enough that they seem to defeat us in every conflict? Must they also torture the men they hold prisoner? They're sadistic fiends, the lot of them!"

Except for medication, she knew what her father would do. As she cleansed the wounds, a softer expression crossed her face.

"But not Stanfield. He would not do this. And not Red McClanahan," she murmured. "Surely they would not be party to this sort of thing."

fourteen

April 1778

The next day Jeremiah brought Dr. Elliott, whose knowing hands thoroughly examined Matt's battered body. Papa's mouth was a grim line when he sat back on his heels. "Has he been conscious at all?"

"No, Papa. He spoke awhile back but it was delirium. How badly is he hurt?"

"His heart is strong. The pulse is a bit fast. It's a wonder he didn't die of fever. I brought some ointment. You must rub it in carefully, like this."

Dipping his finger into the jar, he touched the abrasions lightly, but generous portions of the ointment soon covered the wounds. "That's the best thing we have available at the moment."

Merry reached to wipe Matt's brow with a cool cloth. She gasped as a hand caught her arm. Matt's glassy eyes riveted on her face.

Dr. Elliott swiftly knelt beside them. "Matt?"

"Becka. You've got to help me. Take this to one of our men. See that it gets to Jim. You understand?"

"Matt, it's all right. You're safe now. Just lie back and rest," Dr. Elliott urged.

Matt's hand clamped so tightly, Merry winced, and the stark vacancy in his eyes terrified her. Dr. Elliott eased his son back to the pallet. Merry and her papa exchanged glances.

"Who is Becka?" Merry asked.

"Evidently someone important to Matt. Here now, Son, it's all taken care of. Just try to sleep. That will help you heal." The doctor gently patted Matt's shoulder as he sagged into unconsciousness again.

"I'll be back as soon as I can. Keep me informed. And, Merry, whatever happens, do not come yourself. They have been closely watching me ever since McClanahan was taken." Dr. Elliott gathered her into his arms for a brief embrace, then retrieved his bag and trudged up the stairs.

Nell brought some warm broth and, between them, they got a small amount down Matt's throat.

Aunt Mina joined them. "Merry, I had a full night's sleep. Let me sit with Matt while you go up and try to rest."

"I wish I could talk to Caroline. Couldn't I have Jeremiah take me—"

"You are not to leave the house, Meredeth. Those are orders from your papa. Now go get some sleep, my dear. You will need it if we are to bring your brother out of this."

"Yes, Aunt Mina. Thank you."

Curled up on the window seat, Merry sat gazing out at the colors of spring adorning the world. The call of a loon off in the distance brought back memories.

"Will, please come back. I'm so frightened for Matt, for Papa, and all of us. It is like being caught in a terrible storm that never ends. I miss you so."

She reached for her Bible and opened it to her favorite bookmark. Her voice was low as she read the words she so often turned to, Hebrews 13:5 and 6.

" '. . .For he hath said, I will never leave thee, nor forsake thee. . .The Lord is my helper, and I will not fear what man shall do unto me.' "

"Even Hastings," she reminded herself. "I do believe, Lord, but it is frightening. Help us to put our trust in You and continue on our life road bravely."

❧

Except for Dr. Elliott's visit, no one came calling, not even Caroline. Strange, Merry mused, leaning her head back against the wall. There had been so many visitors before. She rubbed her weary arms. Matt often thrashed about and it was hard to keep him on the pallet during those shows of strength. He was so worried about this Becka, whoever she was. Merry stretched to relieve cramped muscles, then glanced at her brother. Sweat poured from his brow down his gaunt features. When she lifted the coverlet, she found moisture beading on his chest and shoulders. Was he worse or was his fever breaking? She bent to soothe him with cool cloths.

"Matt, can you hear me?" she asked.

His entire body convulsed, then lay limp.

"Matt!" Fear nearly choked her. Swiftly she checked his heartbeat and pulse.

His eyes flickered several times before two blue-green circles stared back at her in shock. "M–Merry?"

"Yes, oh yes, Matt," her voice trembled. She reached to wipe her tears from his arm. His skin was cool!

"What are you doing here?" he asked shakily.

She giggled like a child. "I am trying to take care of you, that's what I'm doing."

His puzzled regard moved from her to the cramped hidey-hole, the wooden shelves protruding beyond, and finally the stairwell.

"Where. . .? Jim! Did we make it to Mrs. Clairmont's then?"

"Yes, though you gave me a fright, falling so dramatically, face down on the grass. Matt, when I got that package, I thought you were dead. By the way, did you send that wild man on horseback to deliver it? He near ran Fair Lady and me down!"

Matt managed a wry grin before he replied in a strained attempt at conversation. "I thought I was as good as dead! They had the tavern surrounded. Somehow Becka must have gotten me up the stairs to her room and hidden me. Bless her heart and her quick mind. I lost consciousness. When I awoke, I was in a wagon, trying hard not to black out again. The rickety wheels hit every rut in the road. Then I vaguely recall being on a ship. . .or maybe I dreamed that."

"Probably a prison ship. The Brits have several."

"No, I don't think so. Those two men cared about me. They couldn't have been the enemy. Next thing I knew I was in Boston and some of Washington's men put me in a small cabin and told me to lie low. Someone was to pick me up, but the Redcoats found me and took me to prison. It was a nightmare. I was there for quite a while."

He rubbed a hand over his face. A slow, tentative smile almost changed him into the Matt she knew so well. "Then one night a rock came flying through the window. Somehow Jim Hanks located me. He told me to be ready, he'd come for me the next night. There was a fire in the trash at the back of the building. While all the guards raced to quench that, Jim climbed through the window, released me, and half-carried me out to his horse. What a wild ride that was! He dumped me off and told me to get inside the house quickly. Then he took off immediately. I don't remember anything after that."

"Jim sent word he was bringing me something," Merry informed him. "I was to take care of it for him. I thought he meant another note for Washington. Oh, bless Jim Hanks for bringing you back to us! We didn't know what had happened to you."

"What do you mean you expected a note for Washington?" His startled expression erased the grin from her face.

"I've been delivering messages now and then," Merry said.

Matt reached for her, but his energy faded and he fell back to the pallet, panting. "Merry, you shouldn't be involved in all this! You're a. . .a. . ."

"I'm a woman, just like a good many others," she replied, her chin tilted up.

He sighed. "Yes, I guess you are, but I don't like to think of you in danger."

"Just who is this Becka you keep talking about?"

His grin returned. "Another Patriot, daft as you. I hope you get to meet her someday. You two will get along just fine."

"Probably we will. Which reminds me, I think you and

Will should be good friends, also."

"Will who?"

"Will Castleton. He's the man I'm going to marry."

"Hmmm. That name sounds familiar for some reason. Do I know this future brother-in-law?"

"No. He's from Boston. He and his late uncle own a shipping line. Jim Hanks knows him well. Will's in Boston right now. His uncle died and he had to go back. The last time he was here he talked to Papa, then proposed to me."

"Do you love him, Merry?" Matt asked softly.

"Oh, yes, very much."

"Then I'm happy for you."

Nell appeared on the stairs. Her worried frown alerted Merry and Matt to the world around them. "Dela and I'm goin' to have to close this quick. You two stay there and play mum."

The shelves were pushed in place, closing them off. They heard the scrape of barrels heaved across the cellar floor. Then total silence enveloped brother and sister like a funeral shroud. They stared at each other, grasping hands. For what seemed like hours they waited, hardly daring to breathe, while heavy feet pounded on the stairs and doors slammed. Quiet returned almost secretly, a little at a time.

At last a whisper reached them. "Stay hidden awhile. That was Brits and some of them are still in the yard. They're standing there talking."

It was another eternity before barrels and shelving were pulled back. Mrs. Clairmont's pale visage peered at them. "They've gone at last, thank the good Lord."

Later that night, a subdued group gathered around the table in darkness. Dr. Elliott, Jeremiah, Jim Hanks, and Caroline joined them.

"What are we to do? That man is determined to arrest one of us." Dr. Elliott put all their thoughts into words.

"I probably shouldn't be telling this," Jim spoke up, "but we heard the northern campaign is going in our favor.

"One day Burgoyne was on the march when a whole contingent of men appeared, claiming to be Loyalists. They carried German guns just like the Redcoats and had papers of introduction. Burgoyne was overjoyed to get them. He sent them to guard his rear."

Jim chuckled as he continued, "They came to a wooded area and Brits began falling like birds on a fence. About a dozen men waited in the trees ahead. They knocked out the whole center section of the Redcoats, including two officers. When the Brits turned to see what had happened, they looked right into the rifles of Daniel Morgan's men. They were Loyalist, all right. . .loyal to the Patriots. That's only one confrontation. Our men practice a few Indian tactics, and the Redcoats are losing a lot of men up north."

"Is that why Howe is going to Boston?" Elvira asked.

"He was supposed to go to New York. Clinton and Burgoyne were to join him and hold out there. Well, Howe delayed, Burgoyne was near wiped out, and Clinton is still in winter camp. It's been misunderstandings and bungles throughout their army. Also, the Indians they hired have not been paid as promised and they are rebelling."

"Where do you think Howe will go?" Dr. Elliott queried.

"Washington's had some victories in New Jersey. I think Howe will go to New York. That's why Hastings is so set on getting his hands on Merry before he leaves, Doc."

"Is there any way we could get her out of town for a while, to protect her?"

Jim answered slowly, thoughtfully. "If we could get her past the guards to the river, I know a man who has a canoe. He could take her upriver at night. From there I could get her to one of our safe houses, then to New Jersey."

Dr. Elliott's deep voice broke the silence. "I think I can get her past the guards."

Everyone looked to him in surprise.

"I know of a secret tunnel that will take her to the river. Could your man be waiting there in a boat?"

Jim leaned forward in excitement. "That sounds good to me!"

"Merry, you go pack and bring a change for Matt. We can't let Hastings find him, either."

Merry dashed upstairs. The doctor left to see Anders, the brewer. Jim and Caroline went to get a buggy. Elvira hugged Aunt Mina, then sent Nell to pack some food.

Soon, they had Matt in one of Mr. Clairmont's suits. By the time Merry was dressed and a small carpetbag had been packed with a few extra clothes, Dr. Elliott came bustling in. "A boat will be waiting for them at the exit of Anders's tunnel," he said. "The brewer has his hounds on guard as a precaution."

When Jim and Caroline drove up with the buggy, the entire group gathered to wish the refugees well.

Dr. Elliott took a deep breath and smiled. "Before we leave, let's clasp hands and ask the Lord's blessings on those who leave us and those who remain."

He reached for Merry's hand and Matt's. The circle formed, quiet but for the doctor's soothing words.

"Lord God, we must part from these we love for sometime. Thank You for Your promise to be with us. Keep us close in our hearts and thoughts, though we may be far apart. Watch over us, guide us in the right directions, and in ways pleasing to You. Thank You, Lord, for all the love and mercy You pour out on Your people. In the name of Jesus, Amen."

"Dr. Elliott, can you drive?" Jim asked. "I have to set things up on the other side."

"I'd be happy to. Here, Merry, help me boost Matt up." Once his son was settled, Dr. Elliott climbed in and pulled his daughter up to his other side. "If we should be stopped, I stand the best chance for getting us through as far as Anders's place."

Matt and Merry squeezed themselves into the corners, tugging their hats low. The horses took off at a good clip. They passed a troop of soldiers, but a glance at Dr. Elliott produced only a shrug among them.

Anders was waiting with a lit lantern. Swiftly the family hustled through his office and into the tunnel. The door closed behind them and two dogs sat as sentinels when the camouflage was put in place.

It seemed they descended for miles. The lantern at last promised a level path, and soon they trudged upward. Twice they halted to let Matt rest. He leaned heavily on the doctor's arm and Meredeth's shoulder. Finally, they reached a short flight of steps where two more dogs sniffed at their heels. A quiet command from Dr. Elliott sent the hounds pushing out a small door.

They stopped to listen. Water licked the shore; a minute creak of oars and the shush of a beached boat encouraged them. The doctor leaned out far enough to insure they met friend, not foe. Dr. Elliott gave them a last hug, then helped them into the boat. Their bag was tossed in and a hefty push set them afloat.

"Now I know how the parents of baby Moses felt," Dr. Elliott said to himself.

By the time they reached the bend in the river, they saw only Papa's white face at the tunnel exit. The canoe smoothly caught the current and left the city behind them. A short time later, the boatman turned into the bank on the far side of the river and tied up to a huge oak. He shouldered Matt up the bank to a cluster of brush. There was not so much as the glow of a candle. All they heard was the croak of frogs, the gentle murmur of water, and Matt's labored breathing. That also quieted.

There they huddled for a long time, not daring to speak. Their minds imagined all the things that could have gone wrong. Where was Jim? Did he get out safely?

Merry did not at first catch the small sounds approaching them, but the boatman stiffened to alertness. His keen eyes searched the fields and the river.

Somebody stumbled, falling into them. The old man grabbed

the intruder, jerking the body away from the two huddled at the foot of the oak. A long, lanky figure folded into a compact heap nearby. It was Jim!

"Thanks, Haggis. It was impossible to see clearly in all this brush. Come here to me, darlin'."

"Whew! You near scared me out of my boots," the boatman whispered as he lowered the body he held to Jim's lap.

"Caroline! What are you doing here?" Merry gasped.

"At the moment I am sitting in my future husband's lap. Surprise!"

"You're getting married?" was all Merry could think to say.

Jim grinned. "I'm being transferred north to Boston. Didn't want to leave her here with monsters like Hastings around, so I proposed and she accepted and here we are. You two can be chaperones."

"I left a note for Mama," Caroline added. "She plans to stay with Aunt Bertha. They don't really need me, but I figured this fellow needed a wife to take care of him. Will said you two were to settle in Boston and that way we can be close."

"You know I wish you the best," Merry smiled broadly. "I will enjoy having a friend nearby, too."

Haggis rose and stretched. "It looks clear as fer as I kin see. Best we git agoin' afore someone else comes along."

In mute agreement they all squeezed into the boat. Jim helped Haggis paddle and they set out, keeping close to the bank. The only living things abroad seemed to be night animals. On the distant bank, a group of riders cantered by. . . probably a British patrol. They took no notice of the small craft tucked in the shadows.

"Haggis," Jim spoke softly, "start watching for a narrow bit of land reaching out into the river. There'll be a tree hanging over the water."

A grunt from the old man was the only answer, but all eyes focused on the left bank.

Jim saw it first. He tapped Haggis's arm and pointed ahead. Merry realized she was shivering, no doubt as much from fear as the cool air. They were so close to success.

"Now listen, each of you," Jim said. "No talking. Just follow me."

He led them unerringly through woods and meadows, past a group of horses in one narrow valley.

"The Brits must not have been here," Jim remarked. "They've been confiscating every horse they could find."

In the distance, a small tongue of smoke rose from the chimney of a farmhouse. With practiced cunning, Jim led his friends past the fringes of civilization and into deep woods, where they finally stopped to rest.

"I think I recognize that house. Stay out of sight while I check it out."

He came back with a broad grin on his face. "I should earn a medal. Wait 'til you see what I have." With a dashing bow, he laid out a cloth filled with a round of cheese, a loaf of freshly baked bread, and some dried grapes.

Matt managed a crooked grin, but he was almost too exhausted to eat. With exchanged looks, the others agreed it was time to stop and let him recuperate a bit. Merry closed her eyes. Ummm. Never had warm bread and cheese tasted so good. Within minutes she, Matt, and Caroline were fast asleep. Jim kept guard for several hours before waking them.

"We should get farther from town before we hole up for the day. If we travel at night there's less chance we'll be seen."

The food must have given Matt new strength for he managed to walk by himself for several hours. Low, scudding clouds brought a light rain that persisted, and Jim took advantage of the miserable weather to get his small group into the wooded hills. There they found a cave where it was safe to build a fire, and by nightfall all were dry and warm. Jim returned from a hunt with two rabbits hanging from his belt.

"I think each of us should take a blanket, just in case the rain continues. I'll carry Matt's. We can't take a chance on any of us getting sick. There shouldn't be too many folks out tonight. As long as we keep to the brushy areas or thick woods, there's little chance of running into a Brit patrol. Keep close, now. This is rocky ground," Jim warned.

Matt walked closer to his sister. "Tell me more about this man you love so much," he demanded.

"He is an Englishman who came to the colonies a few years ago to help his uncle run a shipping line. We met when he was riding one day and wandered onto our land. He helps Jim Hanks at times and has been very helpful to us in various ways. I love him, Matt, with all my heart."

Matt grinned. His little sister had become a grown woman when he was not looking. Shaking his head, he put an arm around her shoulders.

"I guess a lot of things have happened to both of us. We need time to catch up. I want to tell you about the love of my life, too."

"I'm looking forward to that. This Becka you mentioned several times sounds like a brave woman," Merry replied with a spark in her eyes.

Jim led them through a dense stand of trees, then halted as they came to a fenced meadow. A hound howled in the distance; it was answered by another much closer. Suddenly a low, menacing growl made Merry and Caroline jump. The animal was some forty feet away, its eyes bright, glaring at them. It stalked closer, a deep rumbling in its throat.

fifteen

"Move slowly back to that tree just behind you, ladies. Grab a low branch and climb fast. I'll hold its attention. Go now!" Jim ordered.

Matt urged the women up into the tree, then tried to pull himself up, calling, "Come on, Jim!"

Jim bolted. Caroline and Merry clung together as the dog attacked the base of the tree, snarling and jumping. Jim tugged Matt higher until they were all out of reach.

"That was close," Merry whispered. "What do we do now?"

"Wait for the beast to get tired and go home," Jim muttered.

Caroline looked at him in astonishment. "How long will that be?"

"How do I know? We'll just have to wait. If it can't reach us, it will look for better game."

The dog circled the tree, trying on all sides to leap high enough. When that failed, it sat on its haunches and glared at them.

"He's not going away, Jim," Caroline mumbled.

"Be patient. We can wait it out. Oh no," Jim groaned, "there's another one coming!"

"What are we going to do now?" Merry asked when the second dog trotted up to nuzzle around the tree.

"Wait a minute. Maybe the second beast will talk the other one into going for better game," Jim insisted.

Caroline humphed. "And maybe we can pretend we are birds and fly."

"You've got to learn to trust me, Caroline, or how are we going to make a marriage work?" Jim retorted.

Silence reigned for a few minutes.

"Ha! I've got it!" Jim informed them. "Leave it to the master spy. I'll save you, my beauties, and you, too, Matt. When I say the word, run as fast as you can."

He stood precariously on the limb, holding to the trunk with one arm. His free hand reached for his belt.

"The rabbits." Merry grinned at Caroline, who clutched the tree desperately. "He's right. They're probably hungry."

Jim removed the first animal and dangled it to get the dogs' attention. Then, with all his might, he flung the rabbit away. Howling in unison, the two hounds raced after the enticing smell.

"Now everyone get ready to go!" Jim ordered, sending the second rabbit in a neat arc even farther away.

"Good shot!" Matt exclaimed as he started down the trunk.

"Ladies, it is time to retreat." Jim looked pleased with himself, jumping to the ground and bowing. "Climb down, Caroline. I'm right beneath you."

Merry turned to look at her friend who stared into space, still clinging to the tree as if her life depended upon it. "Caroline, we've got to go before those dogs come back!" But Merry might as well have been talking to the wind. She tugged at the dazed young woman's arm, but it made no difference.

Jim's voice came softly, beguiling, "We must go, Caroline. Come to me, love. You can do it."

"Jimmmm! What if I fall?"

"Then I'll catch you. I've got muscles you haven't seen yet, young lady. Now get down here where you'll be safe. . . with me."

Without a reply Caroline squeezed her eyes shut and slid off the limb. Fortunately, Jim had his arms out to encourage her.

"Umphhh!" he sputtered as they both went down in a heap.

Merry quickly climbed down, shaking her head at their antics. They were both gasping for breath, but Jim laughed in spite of his battered body.

"May I hope you will always obey me as well, my sweet almost-bride."

Merry darted after Matt, who set a surprising pace. When they reached the river, Jim leaned against a tree to get his breath.

"I don't think the beasts followed us. You three stay here while I reconnoiter the area."

Noiselessly, he disappeared. Now that the emergency was over, Matt fell to the ground, bracing himself against a tree. Merry went to offer him a drink from their water bag. Her brother swallowed once, then closed his eyes, snoring slightly. Merry and Caroline kept watch.

"Our luck's in tonight." Jim's confident voice raised their spirits immensely. "There's an old, abandoned shack about a hundred yards from here. Fur traders used it years ago to overnight when they worked their trap lines. It's not much, but it will keep the wind off. We may have more rain soon."

Matt was hoisted to his feet with effort. "I can make it that far. Let's go before my legs turn to mush again."

Their shelter was not very promising. The roof was in bad shape; hopefully it would not leak. One shutter was missing and they would have to cover that window. Jim looped his blanket in one hand and swept out the debris, evidently left by some small animals seeking refuge. An old piece of canvas served to cover the window.

"Now," he said, "if we each wrap up in a blanket, we should keep reasonably warm."

Jim dug into a bag he had brought from the farm the day before. Grinning, he handed each one an apple. "Try not to think of those hounds eating our supper. Give me the water bag. I'll go fill it."

Eagerly, Meredeth and Caroline accepted the fruit. "At the moment, all I long to do is sleep, but this does taste good," Merry said.

Caroline stared at Jim's retreating figure. "Isn't he wonderful? I simply couldn't let him go without me. I do love him so."

"I pray Will is safe. I wonder if he is on his way back by now."

"Maybe Jim knows where he is. Why don't you ask him in the morning?"

Merry nodded, too tired for further conversation. She took a blanket and wrapped it snugly around Matt, who had fallen asleep with the uneaten apple in his hand. Merry slipped the fruit into his pocket, then reached for her own coverlet. She and Caroline snuggled together for warmth.

A storm roared across the land; startling cracks of thunder and lightning, like evil fingers, grasped at the trees.

Merry sat straight up, breathing hard. Matt lifted his head groggily, his face a twisted mask of pain. "Becka?" he whispered, reaching out.

"Matt, you're here with Jim, Caroline, and me."

"Oh, yes. I remember. I'm worried sick about her, Merry. Jim has heard nothing of her since that night. None of the men have seen her. She could be dead for helping me! If anything happened to her. . .Merry I love that girl."

"I feel the same way about Will. He should have been back weeks ago. But we can't help them now. We have to trust the Lord to watch over them, Matt."

Tears came then in a flood and Matt gathered her into his arms. "Sis, are you sure Will's working for the Patriots? He is British, after all."

"He came from England, but so did our family, Matt. He is one of us. I truly believe that," Merry insisted.

"He loves you, Merry. He'll be back," Caroline spoke softly from the darkness.

The storm moved on and, in the sudden quiet of the cabin, they all slept again. Dawn brought a heartening promise when Jim strode in the door, his face beaming in triumph. He held up a string of fish that made them all forget their problems for a time. In a sheltered crevice of rock, they built a fire and hung their breakfast on sharpened sticks over it. Nothing had ever tasted quite as good!

When they were done eating and everything was packed, Jim urged them to hurry. "I've seen no British patrols this far east, but we must keep a sharp lookout. The safe house is only a few hours away."

There was plenty of cover. Evergreens grew thickly around them until they reached a summit overlooking a deep valley. There they rested, sharing the last of the water.

"Do you truly think the Brits might retreat?" Caroline asked.

"I wouldn't say retreat, exactly. If Washington has many more victories, the Brits won't be able to hold the land they have taken. I think they will give up Philadelphia and concentrate on holding Boston and New York. The harbors there are the best mooring, safe from storms."

"How about Baltimore," Merry wondered.

"That would be too far from the rest of their troops," Matt broke in. "Their supply lines would be stretched to the breaking point."

"One thing's sure." Jim frowned as he spoke. "If they move, they could have reconnaissance patrols anywhere from here to Boston. Keep on the alert."

With that warning, Jim urged them to a faster pace. About noon he herded them into a copse of trees and slipped out to scout again. Matt, his energy drained, promptly fell asleep. Merry and Caroline filled the water bags from a nearby stream, then crouched where they had a good view of the surrounding area. Both leaped to their feet when Jim silently came up behind them.

"The conquering hero returns with food for all!" he declared, holding up a good-sized turkey.

"But we heard no shot fired," Caroline exclaimed.

"A gun firing could be heard a long way in these hills. Didn't I tell you? Washington says I can throw a knife better than any in his army. Not that I wish to brag, but. . ." Jim grinned, tying the bird to his pack.

"Oh, of course not." Caroline gave him a big smile.

"How does the Old Fox manage while you are off seeing us to safety?" Matt chuckled.

"He's got Craig and Clark. Those two can run rings around me and never miss a breath. I'm acting confident to hide the feeling someone is following us. Can't explain it. It's only a strange sense of presence. Keep as quiet as possible."

They kept to the woods until a rocky bluff confronted them. Jim signaled them to follow and started up a zigzag animal track. By the time they all reached the top, they were all stumbling on uneven ground. Often, Jim stopped to listen. At last he shinnied up a tree for a better look.

When he leaped to the ground, a satisfied smile filled his face. "We're almost there. Follow me. Matt, if you need a shoulder to lean on, just say so."

A short trek through woods brought them to a small cabin. Its crudely hewn logs sagged in places, but someone had filled the cracks. It looked sturdy enough. Digging a slim metal rod from his pocket, Jim inserted it between the planks of the door; a quick twist of his wrist brought the heavy door swinging outward. His eyes searched the woods carefully as he urged them into the surprisingly clean interior.

A dilapidated table with four ancient chairs took up half the space. One wall offered four bunks complete with blankets. Two more pallets were arranged in one corner near the tiny hearth.

"It shouldn't get too cold tonight. We'd better forego a fire and use blankets. That way no one will notice smoke. Water's in the well just outside the door. I am going to get Nathan. He'll be your guard while I make a thorough search of these woods. Matt, you keep this gun."

"Thanks. The Brits took mine."

"We can keep watch," Caroline offered. "Matt, why don't you lie down for a while. This trek has been hard on you."

The women discovered several knotholes in the shutters, through which they had a fair view of the immediate area.

"Listen to all the birds up here," Merry whispered. "It's almost like being at Cresswick Acres. I wonder. . .will we ever see our homes again?"

"It seems we've been trudging these hills forever. When Jim and I get married, I think I'll talk him into a home in a valley."

They enjoyed the pleasant sounds of the small wildlife, and to pass the time, they called to memory a great deal of their school days. When they were tired of standing, they pulled the chairs close to the window.

It seemed to be hours before they noticed anything other than the local animal life. A sudden silence dominated the space they watched. Both focused eyes and ears as tension tightened.

"Caroline, what's that?"

"I saw it, too. What shall we do?"

"I'd better wake Matt," Merry muttered as she shook his shoulder.

Matt raised himself to one elbow. "Wha—"

"Someone's coming," she spoke in his ear.

In one heave, Matt was on his feet and went to the window. A low, crouching figure sped toward the cabin, using the screen of shrubs to hide. Matt drew the gun Jim left with him and he steadied his hand.

sixteen

"It's Jim. He's back." Matt sagged in relief. Caroline went to open the door.

"Who said there wasn't a rainbow at the end of a storm?" Jim grinned as he dumped cheese, bread, carrots, and apples on the table, then reached to hug Caroline. "And here are some cinnamon rolls and honey cakes. A feast!"

After taking one look at Matt, Jim made a decision. "Matt's wound has opened again. I'd better get him to the hospital tent. It's only about a day's ride north. I brought two mounts for us, my friend. You've been looking green around the gills too long."

"Can't we come with you?" Caroline pleaded.

"That's no place for you, ladies. I'll be back in two days and take you two east to Washington's camp. You'll be a lot safer there. I filled the water bucket as I came in. It's by the door. Caroline, Merry, let me show you something just in case of emergency."

He led them to the table and lifted the worn rag rug. "Watch how I do this now. See this knothole? You lift it this way."

Though uneven ends of wood did not betray a trap door, the planks opened to reveal a ladder. Jim held his lantern to show them a small dugout beneath.

"If anyone else comes, you open this without moving the table. When it's almost closed, pull the rug back to the trap door. This has served us well, even from Indians. It should fool the Brits. You two be as quiet as you can and keep a sharp ear for any noises. I brought Nathan back with me. He's posted right out there where the woods begin. You know I wouldn't leave you with anyone I didn't trust completely."

With a swift hug for Caroline, he hurried Matt out. Merry and Caroline watched through the knotholes until evening shadows devoured the men.

⁂

By afternoon the next day, both Meredeth and Caroline were shivering, either from the cold or apprehension. They huddled together at the table, listening to the raging storm outside.

"I think I know every chink in that wall for memory," Merry said, finally breaking the silence. "Tell me more of the plans you and Jim have made."

Caroline happily covered that topic. They dreamed out loud of things they could do together in Boston. Each mentally planned her wedding, while the rain slashed at the cabin and the crashing thunder tore at the fragile threads of their inner anxiety. Both were pacing the floor when they heard the first shots.

Terrified at the realization of their worst fears, Merry and Caroline slipped under the trap door. There was more gunfire. Angry shouts and the pounding of horses' hooves turned their stomachs inside out. Merry tugged the rug back over the trap door, then closed it firmly. She noticed an iron rod hanging to one side. Carefully she threaded it through two straps on the facing board as further precaution. The women clung together for warmth and support. Both jumped when the cabin door slammed back with wooden thunder. Boots stomped front to back; a window smashed, sending a shower of glass to the floor. The footsteps halted.

"They've been here. Look at this food. Why would they leave it?"

"Someone used this pallet. It's rumpled."

"The water bucket's near full. Could anyone live here?"

"Look around you. There's no wood for the hearth. No cooking pots or clothing. Could it be a camping place for hunters?"

"I tell you she was here. A scout saw four of them climb the bluff. He said she was with them."

Meredeth bit her lip to restrain her gasp. She knew well the man who answered. Caroline looked to her in query, but she received only a shake of her friend's head and an admonishing finger over her lips.

Some of the men tramped out, but two remained, arguing loudly. "But they might come back here! Why can't I set a torch to it?"

"Hear me and hear me well! I make the rules for this force! We go after them now! They couldn't have gotten far. I want those women, do you understand? If we don't find them, we can check this place out for more clues. Besides, think what a beautiful sight it will be, burning at night atop this bluff. All the Rebels within miles will see what we do to traitors! When I say we are finished with this shack, then you can put it to the torch. Now mount up! After them!"

At the sounds of hoofbeats retreating, both women closed their eyes and breathed deeply. Their bodies still shivered; cold hands were stiff from holding each other so tightly. They remained motionless until the birds again began their chirping. Only then did relaxation come completely.

"We've got to get out of here, but let's go slowly. That was Hastings. I trust him no farther than I can throw his horse," Merry advised.

She eased the rod loose, then lifted the trap door an inch at a time. There was no sign of Hastings's men. Cautiously, they climbed up into what was left of the cabin. The door hung sideways from one leather hinge. Glass was everywhere. Shutters were torn off and pallets lay in a heap. Still crouching low, they peeked out a window. They could see no one, but they knew there was no safety here for them.

"Nathan, where are you?" Caroline said softly, her face frozen in a white mask.

A glance outside provided the grisly answer. Nathan lay face down; his body, riddled with wounds, was still.

In a panic of fear, Merry and Caroline raced through woods and small clearings with no thought of destination. They had to get away from Hastings and the cabin that was no longer safe. Only when they reached a well-beaten track did the enormity of their plight stop their frantic haste. Dropping to the ground under a stand of thick pines, they assessed the options while they caught their breath.

"We must try to reach Washington," Caroline insisted. "I have only a vague idea of his location, but we can't stay here."

"Do you think we can find the way by ourselves?" Merry asked.

"We have to, Merry. We're on our own now. Jim won't know where to find us."

Merry lowered her gaze, painfully opening fingers nearly frozen in their grip on a small knife she had grabbed up as they made for the underground hole. "I have this," she said.

"One small knife between us and that brute of a man."

"Caroline, when we began this journey, Matt and I turned our lives over to God. He's the only one Who can get us out of this predicament now. Will you pray with me. . .ask for His help?"

"I've gone to church all my life, Merry, but do you honestly think the Almighty Lord is going to take an interest in two lost women? He has much larger problems on His mind."

"Caroline, when Abram went into a strange country because God sent him there, when David was being hunted down by Saul's army, or when Elijah thought he was the only believer left in his world, did God take a vacation or a nap and refuse to help them? God promised He'd be with them and He kept that promise."

"You truly believe He will bother Himself about us, don't you?"

"Yes, Caroline, I do. Will you pray with me?"

"Well, it certainly can't do any harm."

Eyes bright, Merry clasped Caroline's hands. Bowing her head, she spoke with new energy, as if God had already picked her up in His arms.

"Dear Father in heaven, please hear our prayer and come to

our rescue. Hastings is a powerful man and has many others to help him, but You are far more powerful than any man. You can call hosts of angels to help us. Oh, my Lord, we need Your help desperately. Please look down on us with Your love and mercy. Show us the way to go and please watch over Matt and Jim and keep them safe, too, Lord. We ask it in the name of Jesus, Your beloved Son and our beloved Savior. Amen."

Their eyes met and hope blazed there. Carefully they searched the trees around them and the visible length of the road. There was no sound, no movement; it was as if they were the only two people in this part of the world.

They rose and set out with blade-sharp awareness, moving carefully through the trees. Stealth was the only weapon they had other than the thin knife clutched in Meredeth's hand. She nodded encouragement when Caroline stooped to dislodge a sharp-edged rock from the soil. As their confidence grew, they ran, in the easy lope of an Indian, toward the northeast and Washington.

A minute vibration under her feet slammed Merry to a stop and, without a word, she dragged Caroline into the brush beside the track they followed. Horses pounded closer and they were almost past the bushes where the women hid.

The last rider, though, cantered by with easy grace, and Meredeth gasped at the sight of that well-known profile. She stood and called out in a wavery voice, "Stanfield!"

Caroline jerked her friend to the ground, but not before that last Redcoat slowed and turned.

In a scattering of turf, the first three horsemen pulled up with questioning looks, but Stanfield pointed in another direction and shouted to them, "I thought I saw a deer. We could use some venison for supper. Go on. I'll check it out."

Grinning their approval, the others wheeled their mounts and were soon out of sight. Stanfield waited until he was sure they were gone before he maneuvered his horse into the woods.

"Who called me?" he asked the bushes.

"No, Merry, we don't dare!" Caroline whispered.

But that anxious whisper coaxed Stanfield nearer.

Merry stood, dragging a reluctant Caroline with her. "Stanfield. Help us, please."

His startled exclamation was barely voiced before he was out of the saddle. "Meredeth, what are you doing so far from Philadelphia?"

"Hastings was determined to prove me a spy. We had to leave town, but he had us followed. He almost caught us in a cabin back there."

"So that's why he sent our troop on duty up here in the woods! He was trying to get us out of his way," Stanfield muttered.

"We stayed overnight in a cabin," Merry told him. "There was a man guarding us. They killed him. Hastings's men came storming into the cabin and. . .and. . ." Merry's speech broke into sobs.

Stanfield reached for Merry. Caroline's eyes opened wide, though she said not a word.

"And we were but a mile away!" he exclaimed. "Hush, now. It will be all right. I'll see you to Patriot territory. I know an old woman there. She'll keep you safe until you can notify your family. It's not far. I can still make it back to our camp tonight."

"Will that make trouble for you. . .coming back so late?" Meredeth inquired.

"I'll simply tell them my horse cast a shoe and I had to go to a blacksmith. You and Caroline can ride Thunder. I'll walk alongside. Now, up you go."

As they rode, Merry closed her eyes and thanked the Lord for sending Stanfield. It was far too dangerous on their own. Even if they did not fall into Hastings's hands, other soldiers could cross their trail. Stray women were often molested. She was sure Stanfield was trustworthy.

"I'll keep a sharp lookout, but please stay alert yourselves. Tell me if you see anything out of place or moving," he cautioned.

Darkness closed them in its fist. Every small animal came alive, adding its own rustling to the chorus of strange noises. When they found a stream tumbling over a rocky bed, Stanfield halted and helped them down. Wearily they fell to their knees to drink the chilly water. For a few minutes they sat on the mossy bank, until the quickening wind gave the air a frosty bite.

"Be very quiet," he warned. "I'm going to take a look around."

In an instant, he disappeared. Caroline reached for Merry's hand and held it fast. Faintly, a drunken voice stumbled over the words of a lusty tavern song, making Merry wonder if there were more soldiers camped in these woods.

Stanfield returned on the run, scooped Merry up on Thunder, then reached for her friend. "We must circle an encampment," he whispered, moving them off to the left.

Clouds raced from east to west and fog swirled in uncertain circles around them; they could see only a hand's-breadth away. Tensely they put all their senses to work. Recent rains had left the forest floor wet, deadening the sound of hooves. Their breathing seemed loud in their ears. When Stanfield's horse stumbled, he muttered under his breath and swiftly covered the animal's muzzle with his hands. Then he ran a practiced hand over his mount's foreleg. "It's not a serious injury. Lean close to Thunder. We'll move on slowly," he reported.

There was no change in the sounds from the soldiers and hope fluttered exultantly in Merry's heart. They were going to make it! Ahead of them the woods became sparse. For a fleeting second the moon knifed through the clouds; a silver sliver of light revealed an open meadow and, at the edge of that, a stream danced over jutting rocks.

Meredeth turned to Caroline. "It's beautiful, isn't it?" she whispered.

"Hold!" The major's quiet command hit them like a cold wind.

seventeen

From the meadow, a single rider sped toward Meredeth, Caroline, and Stanfield. There was little cover in which they could hide. He was upon them in seconds.

"Ho, there!" the rider said. "Speak up or you are dead men!"

Stanfield moved a bit forward. "Major Stanfield, Scout and Search Troop. What are you doing in these parts, Hastings?"

"Humph! I go where duty calls. Why are you afoot? Did your mount cast a shoe?"

Merry ducked low over the saddle, bringing Caroline down with her.

Hastings must have caught the movement for he came closer, peering intently at the humped shadow. "By the devil's own luck, you've found some women in this dreary place. How fortunate for you."

"They are but children who are lost. I'm taking them home, just north of here. I know their papa," Stanfield tersely replied.

Hastings's horse sidled close enough to brush Merry's leg and Stanfield jerked his horse away so hard that Thunder bucked at the harsh treatment.

But it was not fast enough and, swift as a rattler, Hastings's hand reached to pull back the hood of Merry's cloak. His breath hissed in triumph. "This is, indeed, a fortunate meeting," he snarled.

Both men drew weapons simultaneously.

"You coward!" Stanfield said with a slap on Thunder's hindquarters. "You would harm your own brother if he got in your way. You will not take these women!" The horse raced away into the trees.

A mocking laugh erupted from Hastings as he dug his spurs in savagely and he charged after Thunder.

Just before Thunder passed Stanfield, Stanfield leaped aside. He leveled his gun and, when Hastings turned to charge again, a bullet cracked Hastings's crazed laughter midway.

With a choke of dismay, Hastings clutched at the reins to retain his seat. His mount slowed as the rider collapsed in his saddle. Seconds later, Hastings tumbled to the ground like a broken puppet. His mount galloped off.

Stanfield saw the riderless horse and set out to check on Hastings, but the dark fog hid him. Swerving in the direction that Thunder had taken, Stanfield charged after the women when a lone shot echoed behind him. He spun, arching in pain, and fell heavily to the rocky trail.

"Oh, God! Get them away from here to safety," Stanfield pleaded as blackness invaded his sight and mind.

It took Merry some time to slow and quiet Thunder. The first gunshot had shrieked through the air behind them, but fear and anger spurred her back the way they had just come. Deadly stillness iced the night as a second report split her anxiety into a dozen haunting thoughts.

"No!" her scream tore the night apart.

"Don't go back," Caroline whimpered. "We daren't go back."

Thunder leaped across the stream. Merry was sure it was the same place but the happy skip of the water had dimmed. An eye-blinking wind rushed at them as if to push them away. Incoherently, Her mind asked only one thing: *Have I led Stanfield to his death?*

Meredeth tossed the reins to Caroline and slid to the ground. Panting, she strained for signs of either man, but there was no body in sight. She glared at the clouds. Why couldn't the moon shine now? One hand jerked the hair from her eyes as she struggled through the brush. When several circles had been completed to no avail, she braced herself against a tree, her chest heaving. She must think this out. Where had they gone?

"Merry, come back. We'll never find him in this darkness."
Caroline's plea went unnoticed.

This was about where she had last seen them, Merry
decided. Who shot first? She would bet it was not Stanfield.
He must have been wounded. The other shot had come fast
upon the first. Hastings's horse was gone. Did that mean he
had left or had dismounted or fallen? Stanfield had not followed them, so he had to be somewhere nearby. She has-
tened again through the trees. He could not have gone far if
he was wounded.

A root caught her foot, throwing her to the ground, and she
reached out a hand to minimize the fall. There. . .there was
another hand! A gun lay beside it! Heart hammering, she
explored the arm, the shoulder, the still-warm liquid pooled
on a broad back. Blood? Her fingers found the face, the tousled hair.

"Stanfield? No! Dear Lord, don't let him be dead!"

Drawing a deep breath, she forced herself to do what must
be done. With shaking fingers, she tore a strip from her petticoat and wadded it over the wound.

Another body fell to the ground beside her. "Is it Stanfield?"
Caroline asked.

"Yes," she bit the word out, filled with helpless fury.

"Where is Hastings?" Caroline persisted.

"I don't know."

Caroline moved away, but Meredeth had no thought for
anything but stopping the flow of blood. Hurrying to the
stream, she soaked another portion of her undergarment and
cleaned the wound as best she could. A memory gave her
sudden hope as she reached into the pocket of her underskirt.

Thank the Lord. The tin of salve she had brought for Matt's
back was still there. She dabbed the salve liberally on
Stanfield's back, then wrapped the wound with another strip
of cloth.

In the dim light of dawn's promise, there was no evidence
of other injuries. His pulse was ragged, but it would do. She

brushed a lock of hair from his forehead. Only then did she become aware of sounds behind her.

"Caroline?" she whispered.

"Stanfield, a traitor? I may not make it back to my men, but you'll not leave here alive, either, Rebel!"

Merry jerked around.

Hastings clung to a tree not ten feet away, a useless leg dangling behind him. His coat, hands, and face were smeared with blood. He propped himself against the tree and took deliberate aim, a satisfied sneer cutting across his face.

Merry closed her eyes. A shot broke through the fog. Then a thin shred of a scream echoed from rock to rock as she collapsed in a heap.

The crash of bodies through the brush claimed Meredeth's wavering thoughts. She opened her eyes wide just as arms caught her up, crushing her to a broad, wool-cloaked chest.

"Thank God we were in time!" Will's voice soothed her. "Jim and I heard you scream. Then we saw Caroline stumbling toward the track. My heart almost died inside me when I saw that gun pointed at you. Oh, Merry! I've never prayed so hard in my life."

Suddenly aware of her attempt to change position, Will held her a few inches from him. "Did that miserable excuse for a man hurt you?"

In response to his intense question, she giggled almost hysterically. "No, he. . .I'm. . .please keep holding me. But it's just that I need to breathe and your heavy cloak was not allowing much air to get through. I thought I would never see you again. Hold me tight, Will, so I know I'm not dreaming."

With infinitely gentle hands, Will lifted her face to his and she felt the tremor that shook him. In wonder, she raised her arms to bring him closer and his mouth claimed hers. Vaguely, they were aware of Jim and Caroline behind them, but the near-tragedy made that moment too precious to share with anyone else.

"My dear heart, we must get away from here. There may be

other Brits in these woods."

Will kept a strong arm around her but started off toward his mount. Merry's sharp "No!" halted them.

"Stanfield!" Merry said. "We've got to get help for him. He tried to protect us and he's badly hurt. Will, we can't leave him here to die!"

"Stanfield? You mean the British officer who took you to that ball?"

"Yes." Meredeth's eyes filled with tears.

"Merry, do you. . .I mean, is he. . .?"

Will set her on her feet. One big hand plowed a path through his hair as he struggled to gain control of himself. When he looked at her again, his bleak expression sent her flying to him.

"He is a friend, Will, only a friend, but I cannot leave him here to die. I cannot."

Eyes closed tightly, he threw back his head and took a deep breath. His voice was low, strained. "He's a Brit, Merry."

"That Brit was almost killed helping us," Merry said.

With a sigh, Will drew her close, tucking her head into his shoulder. His rueful chuckle relaxed her taut muscles.

"All right, my dear. I have you back safely, thanks to him. I shouldn't quibble, even if he is the enemy."

She reached a hand to his cheek. Her words were barely audible. "I do love you, Will."

He heard and lifted her in his arms to hug her properly. After checking Hastings to be sure he was dead, the four of them found Stanfield unconscious, but the bleeding had stopped. Will mounted his horse and Jim carefully hoisted the Englishman up to Will's arms. The women rode Jim's horse while he walked alongside. Swiftly they left the forest and turned in at a small village nearby.

Right at the edge of the buildings, they stopped at a big red barn where a plump, older woman sat on a three-legged stool, milking a cow. At the sight of her visitors, her mouth formed a large O. She leaped up, smiling as Jim approached.

"Aggie, can the ladies stay here while we take this Brit to a place where his men will find him? He did us a favor."

If the good woman had questions, she did not ask. Nodding happily, she ushered Merry and Caroline into her home. With a wave, Will and Jim rode back into the woods. By the time the women had washed and eaten a bowl of oatmeal, the men were back.

"His troop was out looking for him. We found their camp and left him there. Is that your cinnamon oatmeal I smell, Aggie? Could you spare a bowlful for two hungry Patriots?" Jim flashed her his best smile.

An hour later they left, with Merry and Caroline riding behind the men. Jim called back, "I'll bring you some catfish to feast on, Aggie. You're an angel in disguise."

"Oh, go on with you," she flustered when he threw her a kiss.

By midday they reached the Delaware River, twenty miles above Fort Mercer. There, they ferried over to the New Jersey side and, within another two hours, they rode into Washington's camp.

While Jim and Will reported to the general, one of his men escorted Meredeth and Caroline to Kate Stillwell's home, where an unexpected surprise awaited in the parlor.

"Papa and Aunt Mina! What are you doing here?" Merry asked.

"You can't imagine how worried we've been. Mina and I left Philadelphia shortly after the British did. We feared Hastings had found you. Oh, the good Lord be thanked!"

"We had a few delays. The British left Philadelphia, then?"

"Yes, every one of them, including some of the Tories, pulled out the evening of June eighteenth. Rumor has it that Ben Franklin made an alliance with France and he will return soon. According to Major Clark, the English fear an attack by the French. Many of the British troops are going back home. We don't know if Hastings went with them or not."

Meredeth lowered her eyes, her lip trembling. "Hastings is

dead, Papa. When he tried to kill me, Stanfield shot him. Then Hastings shot Stanfield. Just as Hastings pointed his gun at me, Will and Jim came along. They killed him, then took Stanfield back to his camp. I think he will be all right. Stanfield tried to save us Papa. He is a good man."

"I will make inquiries to be sure. I think highly of him, too," Dr. Elliott responded.

"Merry! Look who I found wandering around as if he were lost." Will grinned and stepped aside to reveal the big man behind him.

"Red McClanahan! I can't believe it's truly you. We were so worried when they took you from the hospital. How did you come here?"

"It pleases me to see you, lassie. The British left me fevered in a prison tent when Clinton took his men back to Boston. If Will hadna' come looking for me, I'd be in me grave. He brought me here. You know, 'tis a Rebel, I think, this Scot's becomin'. Mayhap I'll bring me family over."

"It's good to see all of you again. Did Dela and Anna come, too?" Merry asked Aunt Mina.

"Well, of course. I could hardly manage without them, although we could bring very little with us. I'll be happy to get back to our normal life again. Such a hurly-burly time we have had, to be sure."

The call for dinner brought them all together around an extended table. Probably Aunt Mina was the only one who could tell afterward what delicious foods were provided. Everyone else was much too busy enjoying the company.

"Miss Merry, would you like a piece of the cake Ma baked?" a voice asked.

Merry turned a startled face to the little serving wench behind her. "Jesse! You're safely away from the Brits! I feared they had arrested your ma."

"Jim heard Mrs. Stillwell was looking for a cook and he brought us up here. I get to serve sometimes. I'm so glad you got away from that wicked Hastings man."

"He won't hurt anyone now. I'll see your ma a bit later."

Beaming her delight, the child marched back to the kitchen.

When the meal was completed, Will invited Merry out to walk in the garden. Moonlight wrapped it in glowing silver and ebony; a wooden bench beckoned under a latticed rose arbor. When Meredeth was seated, Will knelt beside her.

"I must ask your forgiveness, love," he said.

"Whatever for? For rescuing me?" she asked.

"Of course not that. You see, when I was here before, I mentioned my hopes of marriage and taking you back to Boston with me."

"I shall happily go with you wherever you wish."

"I'm glad, but that's not the problem. Mrs. Stillwell is a dear person, but sometimes she takes things into her own hands and. . ."

Merry's eyes danced as she replied, "What has she done, Will?"

"She's planned our wedding for us. It's to be tomorrow. She has the preacher and all the guests coming."

"Tomorrow?" Meredeth stiffened, a look of horror on her face. "I don't have a gown or any clothes other than these. We haven't had the banns read. How can we be married so quickly?"

Will ducked his head. "You two are much the same size. She wants you to wear her wedding gown and her seamstress is making your traveling clothes and a few other dresses. She said that would do until we reach Boston, where you can have more made."

Merry stared back, glassy eyed. "Tomorrow. What about the banns?"

With a quirky grin he said, "The preacher said it could be overlooked this time in view of the fact that I have to be in Boston in five days to receive my inheritance. Everyone wants us to marry here so they can all attend. Do you mind a terrible lot, my dear?"

She looked lovingly at that worried face. With one hand

she lifted the errant lock of hair, fallen to his forehead, as usual.

"Don't fret yourself. I know few people in Boston. It is better that we marry here."

"Then you will? Wonderful! I want to make you mine as soon as possible, and Mrs. Stillwell has worked so hard to make everything work out well. Tomorrow eve. Oh, love, you are all I ever dreamed of in a wife."

He smiled into her moon-starred eyes and ran fingers over her silvered hair before cupping her face and lifting it for his kiss.

"I love you so much, Meredeth Elliott."

"And I love you just as much, Will Castleton."

"I was so frantic with worry over you being subjected to Hastings's wrath. A British patrol gave us trouble at the Maryland docks. It took far too much time to get loaded again."

"Knowing God was with us and thinking of you were the things that gave me strength when Caroline and I had to strike out on our own," Merry murmured into his collar.

Words got in the way. There was a healing hush while they clung tightly to each other. The Stillwell garden quietly folded its trellised enclosure and stole away, leaving only the entwined shadow defined by moonlight.

eighteen

A bit dazed, Merry looked into the mirror the next eve. Her gown was lovely, tiered lace starred with pearls and crystal baguettes. A creamy white veil was poised to lift down over her face. Papa brought her an armful of flowers with one perfect rosebud tied in the center by silk ribands.

"Papa, it is beautiful. Thank you."

"The rose is from Will. He picked it from Stillwell's garden. Merry, we've had word from Matt. He is much better and should be able to visit us soon. He said to wish you happiness."

Vaguely they became aware of music from below. They descended into a flower-laden foyer and then into the parlor. Merry saw nothing but Will's adoring smile and the strong, steady hand he held out to her. The harpsichord ceased its wondrous melody and they turned to the preacher.

Will's big hand shook as he placed the ring, an oval sapphire, edged with pearls, on her finger. The words were spoken at last, making them one. She smiled up at him, her eyes sparkling with happiness. So intent were they on each other, a small ripple of laughter crossed the room.

The preacher said, for the second time, "You may kiss your wife, young man."

A faint pink shaded his face as he gently drew her into his arms and did just that.

They were quickly surrounded by well-wishers, all gaily talking at once. Much later, after small cakes and a bowl of punch satisfied the guests' appetites, Merry and Will slipped away upstairs to a bedroom prepared for them.

"You are so beautiful," he spoke softly, his fingers playing in her hair, then cupping her face for a long kiss.

"Forgive me, but I much prefer your hair down. I love what

the candlelight does to it." Before he finished speaking, his nimble fingers had loosened all the combs, letting the waving strands fall in a copper-sparked curtain to her waist.

"That's much better. Before I forget completely, Mrs. Clairmont sent you a gift. She said you could carry on now that she has finally admitted she is an older lady. . .not old she insisted, just older."

Will reached into his trunk and pulled out some folded material. Striding to the hearth, he spread out the Starfire quilt onto a woolen rug. Smiling, Merry helped him smooth out the pattern.

"She couldn't have given me a better gift," she said.

"You are the only gift I want," he murmured, pulling her closer. "You are dearer to me than life itself. I can't wait to show you our new home. Uncle Reggie left us his house and also a small retreat by the ocean. By the way, after we send the British back to their island, Jim has agreed to work for me. He's good with figures and I don't plan to spend all of my time at the shipyards. There is an uninhabited small home a few blocks from ours. It will do them nicely until they can afford better. That way you and Caroline will be close."

"Will we ride to Boston?"

"I've hired a carriage. Jim and Caroline can travel with us. There's a lot of beautiful country on the way. I wish I could take you home on one of our ships, but that is not possible at this time. We'll do that later."

"So many perplexing things have happened. I've longed to ask you, but when you put your arms around me, I can't think."

"Questions, hummm? I hope they are about how gloriously happy I am to hold you close again."

"In truth they are much more mundane. How did you know Matt?"

"I suppose a lady's curiosity must be appeased," Will sighed but refused to relinquish his hold on her. "Clark brought him to me. I heard that a pretty redhead had delivered him in a bloody cloak. She begged Clark to get him to safety. He knew I was moored there in the harbor, waiting for a message. You should have seen him carrying Matt up the gangplank with the fussy old doctor running to keep up with them! Matt wavered in and out of consciousness. After about a week, Clark and his men carried him off in a barrel to get him by the Brits who were coming to check out my cargo."

"Matt wasn't sure if he had been on a ship or if he dreamt it. Do you know how they delivered the notes I sent on to Jim Hanks?" she asked.

"Oh, that was one of Jim's cousins. That whole family is involved in Washington's spy system. The boy was just fourteen, but he wanted to help. He was sorry he almost ran you down that day. He feared the Brits had seen him, so he set the horse at too fast a pace, then had difficulty controlling it. When I heard how they were using you to get messages through, I'm afraid I lost my temper. They promised they would not make you a go-between anymore."

Merry's mouth opened again, "Do you think the war will—"

Chuckling, Will promptly covered her lips with his own. When she gasped for breath, he nibbled at her ears and softly murmured, "Enough, wife, we have more important things to do. God alone knows when this war will end. He brought us together and gifted us with each other's love. We can trust our futures to Him."

Will caught her to him and in one fluid movement lowered them to the quilt. Merry soon stopped thinking altogether and simply relished the wonder of their new life in the marriage covenant. That seemed to please Will immensely.

And God smiled.

A Letter To Our Readers

Dear Reader:

In order that we might better contribute to your reading enjoyment, we would appreciate your taking a few minutes to respond to the following questions. When completed, please return to the following:

Rebecca Germany, Managing Editor
Heartsong Presents
P.O. Box 719
Uhrichsville, Ohio 44683

1. Did you enjoy reading *The Starfire Quilt?*
   - ❑ Very much. I would like to see more books
     by this author!
   - ❑ Moderately
     I would have enjoyed it more if _____

     _____

2. Are you a member of **Heartsong Presents**? ❑Yes ❑No
   If no, where did you purchase this book?_____

   _____

3. What influenced your decision to purchase this
   book? (Check those that apply.)

❑ Cover	❑ Back cover copy
❑ Title	❑ Friends
❑ Publicity	❑ Other_____

4. How would you rate, on a scale from 1 (poor) to 5
   (superior), the cover design? _____

5. On a scale from 1 (poor) to 10 (superior), please rate the following elements.

     ___Heroine   ___Plot

     ___Hero   ___Inspirational theme

     ___Setting   ___Secondary characters

6. What settings would you like to see covered in **Heartsong Presents** books?_____

_____

_____

7. What are some inspirational themes you would like to see treated in future books?_____

_____

_____

8. Would you be interested in reading other **Heartsong Presents** titles?   ❑ Yes   ❑ No

9. Please check your age range:
      ❑ Under 18   ❑ 18-24   ❑ 25-34
      ❑ 35-45   ❑ 46-55   ❑ Over 55

10. How many hours per week do you read? _____

Name _____

Occupation_____

Address_____

City_____State_____Zip _____

··········· Presents ·······

Great Inspirational Romance at a Great Price!

Heartsong Presents books are inspirational romances in contemporary and historical settings, designed to give you an enjoyable, spirit-lifting reading experience. You can choose wonderfully written titles from some of today's best authors like Peggy Darty, Sally Laity, Tracie Peterson, Colleen L. Reece, Lauraine Snelling, and many others.

When ordering quantities less than twelve, above titles are $2.95 each.
Not all titles may be available at time of order.

SEND TO: Heartsong Presents Reader's Service
         P.O. Box 719, Uhrichsville, Ohio 44683

Please send me the items checked above. I am enclosing $_____.
(please add $1.00 to cover postage per order. OH add 6.25% tax. NJ add 6%). Send check or money order, no cash or C.O.D.s, please.
    To place a credit card order, call 1-800-847-8270.

NAME _____

ADDRESS _____

CITY/STATE _____ ZIP _____

HPS 2-98